PRAISE FOR

STEVE EVANS

What a delight these stories are to read. Steve Evans captures the humour and hardships, foibles and follies, and so many of those unexpected turns that punctuate our lives. Highly recommended.

~ Craig Cormick, author of *A Funny Thing Happened at 27,000 Feet*, winner of the Queensland Premier's Literary Award

These idiosyncratic tales are tantalising segments of lives. Love stories (which also happen to include murder, abuse, retribution, poignancy, contract-killers, break-ups, comedy, exploitation and an orgy of conflagration) about humans of all ages and backgrounds; each story bearing its own atmosphere, its own world. 'We Like You' is one of the best sci-fi stories I've read, combining future tech with the metaphysical. Strong and diverse storylines told in the fertile, succinct language of a poet ...

~ Rob Walker, author of *Square Pegs*

In a terrifically impressive collection of short short-fictions, Steve Evans takes us on a tour of the metaphorical sinkholes of suburbia. Via his observant eye and febrile imagination, we behold the mischievous and manic, the tawdry and tragic, and more. We come upon familiar scenes that then glow in a broadband delivery of hyper-realism. Second-hand books become a successful stalking strategy. A private letter-burning becomes a communal cleansing. In a final afternoon tea, a potential inheritance is consumed in gold-leaf-infused cakes. A deposit-secured wedding cake, a promised book of window paintings, a normal Bay-City tram ... never arrive.

~ Moya Costello, author of *The Office as a Boat: a chronicle*

EASY MONEY

AND OTHER STORIES

STEVE EVANS

TRUTH SERUM PRESS

BP#00081

Truth Serum Press
32 Meredith Street
Sefton Park SA 5083
Australia

Email: truthserumpress@live.com.au
Website: http://truthserumpress.net
Truth Serum Press catalogue:
http://truthserumpress.net/catalogue/

Cover design © Matt Potter
Front cover wedding dress drawing copyright © Clker-Free-Vector-Images
Back cover hand and money bag drawing copyright © OpenClipart-Vectors
Author photograph copyright © Martin Christmas and used with permission

ISBN: 978-1-925536-81-2

Also available as an eBook
ISBN: 978-1-925536-82-9

Truth Serum Press is a member of the
Bequem Publishing collective
http://www.bequempublishing.com/

To those who love

without reserve

CONTENTS

RALPH

'You'll want Ralph, of course.'

Harry leant an elbow on the roof of the car and peered in at me.

Did I? Did I want that fur-tangled, manic lump of stupid affection? This was just Harry wishing aloud again, as if simply saying something would make it so. He kept on staring. Perhaps that furrowed brow was meant to show he was sharing the load, doing some of the hard thinking for me. But it was really only trying to nudge me towards what he saw as the inevitable. Yes? I thought of cartoons at matinee movies, and the sinister will of villains indicated by the terrible force of hypnotic, dotted thought-rays spearing across the screen towards a hapless victim.

'Ralph?'

'Ralph.'

'Oh.'

I rubbed my cheek thoughtfully and made a little smacking sound with my lips; one of those, 'Gee, this is kind of hard' noises I'd heard Harry use too many times. I let the word sit there. I wanted to make Harry speak before I did.

'I've got his bowl and lead here. I can pop them in the car right now. Come on, boy!'

He whistled to Ralph, who lay in the shadow of a ruined geranium bush near the edge of the front lawn. Ralph lifted his rump from the ground. His eyes widened and his jaw opened as if for another game of catch. Harry smiled encouragingly at Annie in the front seat beside me. She did not respond, maybe curious to wait and see how this conversation between her estranged parents would work out.

'Harry, let me get this straight. You think I should have Ralph.'

'Of course. Now that you're moving back here to Melbourne.'

'Mmm. When I took the contract job interstate last year and said I was shifting there with Annie, you got an injunction that stopped me taking her. You thought that would make me give up on a rare chance for my kind of work and stay here, right? All so you could go on just seeing your daughter every second weekend, playing Nice Dad. It was only ever about your convenience, not her well-being, and you know it.'

'It wasn't like that. You had her all the time as her mother, Trish, but how would she get to see me if you two went interstate? I was thinking of her, needing to see me, her father.'

'Bullshit. I offered you more access days than you've ever had, extended breaks on school holidays and other times, and I'd arrange all the travel and pay for it, but I guess that was too hard for you. Occasional weekends are so much easier, aren't they, with me as the full-time parent just a few suburbs away?'

'You have such a cruel streak.'

'Have I? That damned interim court order not only said she couldn't leave the state but that I couldn't either. What a stuff-up! It was so dumb, and it was a legal first, even if it was unintentional. I didn't want to be a legal first, Harry. Thank God they eventually relented about keeping me tied to this crap city, anyway.'

'It got fixed. You shouldn't complain.'

'They still insisted that she couldn't go with me. You played a horrible game of bluff, bidding your own flesh and blood, and treating me like an enforced baby-sitter on a leash. I wanted her with me, but you went too far.'

'It wasn't personal.' His stern expression froze. Here was the forceful, resolute Harry; a 'don't mess with me' Harry. 'You're not all sweetness and light yourself.'

Of course it had been personal, every excruciating legal inch of it. Ralph ambled towards Harry's lowered voice but was distracted by the sound of a bird in the shrubbery and ambled off to investigate that instead.

'Ralph is Annie's dog, Harry. You only decided to look after him to shore up the sympathy vote originally, anyway, to get Annie to keep coming to you on weekends. Don't fob him off now I'm back and you think you've won the war.'

'God, you're hard.'

'I've had a good teacher.'

'He's tearing up my garden,' Harry said, as if that was supposed to commend Ralph to me and my own little square of lawn.

I gazed at Harry while his face contorted. Which expression would he choose next? Did he really expect me to take the dog? Or was it just another 'poor me' appeal: poor me having to care for this rampaging beast; poor me landed with all this extra responsibility; go on, you have to help poor me here. Well, I'd end up with a daughter to mind, which was fine with me, but a bloody great dog as well, plus going back to the old arrangement where I have an ex who doesn't care and comes around to gloat and play bloody word games in my driveway when he does bother to pick her up. Poor Harry? My heart was bleeding.

'I only took him as a favour, while you sorted things out with your move.'

'You took Ralph because Annie wanted him, because it got her on side. That and the new clothes and all the toys and the fast food and letting her stay up late watching her own new TV. You can't just spit out the bits you don't like.'

'It's not my dog.'

If Ralph had discernible eyebrows I think they would have gone up at that one. Reduced to an 'it,' too. Ralph, though, chewed intently on a lump of broken rhododendron.

'Annie would like him to be with you, Trish. God knows why, but she thinks it would be good for the two of you.'

Still Annie did not speak from her seat next to me. I had expected a comment of some kind but there was nothing.

Then my eye was caught by a movement at the front window of the house. A woman's hand at the corner of the curtain. Lonely Harry, 'I'll never find anyone else' Harry, had a partner after all.

I reached back and opened the rear door of the car. Ralph dashed inside and sat bolt upright up on the seat in an instant with goofy eagerness written all over his face. I started the engine and reversed into the street. We were halfway down the block when Annie finally spoke.

'Cheryl doesn't like Ralph, Mum. She says he eats Missy's food and Missy has special food and Ralph shouldn't eat it.'

Cheryl? Missy? I braked. I turned and looked at her. Six years old, her calm face gazing forward through the windscreen. She trusted my driving more than I did. Ralph panted in the back and started circling noisily for a good lying position. The end of upholstery as we know it.

'Cheryl says Ralph is a mongrel and Missy is pedigree and it's her or Ralph. She says one of them has to go.'

Still she looked straight ahead. I lifted my foot off the brake pedal and began driving again, anything I could say momentarily bottled up by anger.

She suddenly pointed outside with excitement. 'There it is! That's the shop! That's where it is. Dad says I can have a new dress from in there, but I'm not allowed to say to you. It was if you took Ralph, and it's a beautiful dress, Mum. It's got lace.'

Her little head swivelled as we passed the display window. I saw the dress there, right in the front, and my heart sagged. It was bad enough this bargain he had with her, but why that dress? Even with the glimpse I had managed as we drove by I had seen the cut of it and the ribbon at the waist. It was my own wedding dress in miniature.

'That's all right, isn't it, Mum? I can see Ralph when I come to visit you — can't I, Ralph?'

Ralph heard. He rose and flopped his big head between the front seats, rolling his dumb eyes up at us. I grated up a gear.

'Of course, Annie. We'll be waiting.'

Sucked in. A year away in another city, trying to make money to get the family — well, me and Annie — back on our feet, and the dog conspiracy was already entrenched. I gritted my teeth. I'd half expected it but told myself to be positive, to imagine better. And I would have fumed over it, despite my self-talk, except Ralph had something else in store. When we parked in front of my little rented house and I flung the rear door of the car open, Ralph jumped out, loped onto the footpath and around the corner of the street and didn't come back.

The neighbourhood streets grew dark as Annie and I traipsed together past houses and through both of the local parks, all the while calling out Ralph's name. We looked down driveways and even behind a small group of shops in case he was fossicking among the bins there. Annie began to fret that someone might have stolen him. I couldn't imagine the appeal of that big galumphing creature I but didn't say so. Then she was convinced that he had been hit by a car or truck and was cringing in a gutter somewhere with broken ribs and blood at his mouth. She always had a good imagination. I soothed her on that account too, though I had also privately conjured similar images and begun to worry on her behalf.

Annie panicked then and that made me panic, and we fussed our way around the district for three hours without finding him. There was no sign of the beast that she loved so much and I began to feel sorry for him as well as Annie.

We returned home in what I promised Annie would be just a short respite with a cup of hot chocolate before venturing out again. We had just slumped onto the couch when the phone rang. Harry with a dark, irritated voice.

'You bitch,' he hissed, 'you sent him back!'

I heard Ralph's happy panting in the background, that blissfully innocent doggy racket.

'No, Harry,' I cooed, 'he loves you. Ralph is man's best friend.'

Behind Harry's frantic complaints, I heard something else, some kind of a weird and shrill duet in a series of discordant dips and crescendos. Eventually, I realised it was the voice of a woman and some other animal shrieking together like banshees. I hung up the phone.

'Annie,' I said, 'get your coat. We're going out for dinner!'

EMMA WAITING

She's the heaviest thing in the room, in the house. The air outside moves more slowly around this slightly run-down weatherboard than the others in the street. She is pulling everything in towards her, the dark centre. Dark despite the white figure she has become, she's the wraith in the half-shadowed upstairs room where nothing moves for hours except her eyes, and nothing escapes those. Emma's mother is dying and she is taking her time about it, as if she'd been preparing for it all her life.

Here is a kind of nunnery for one, the still woman on the iron bed by the window, a member of a silent order. Her cat visits to sit on the sill and share the view of the street below; its look as grave, as sombre as her own. Sometimes Emma joins them and the three stay a while, unspeaking in the dappled afternoon light reaching through the trees. Then Emma goes down the stairs to make tea.

Emma began to leave a note pad at the bedside when her mother's voice grew weak and she began to sleep more often during the day. Emma would come into the room and walk quietly to the bed, sometimes finding the pen and paper untouched for days. Then there would be a short note about something her mother had seen in the street, or a few items to add to her shopping. Three weeks ago she picked up the pad to read her mother's latest request: 'cat food, fresh roses, Charlie's wedding'. That was when her mother began to intermingle shopping hints with moments of her life that she'd distilled to a phrase — the pallid doll remembering, deconstructing. Gradually, the messages grew shorter and less frequent, eventually reducing to a single word at a time.

One afternoon Emma picked up the pad as usual. Her mother lay still, those dull eyes watching without reaction as Emma read. The note was brief again: 'apple'. That was all it said. This did not mean that Emma should buy apples or that she should bring one to her mother. Emma had learnt by then. It was a meditation, a summoning of the idea of the thing. Her mother was bringing them back in her own time and order. Apple, linen, milk, ice. Dealing with them. 'Charlie is my darling,' she used to sing, but not anymore. Straw, fig, silk.

Now Emma looks at the day's chosen word and closes her eyes for a moment. She knows her mother's eyes are open and she also knows that the two of them are thinking together, about 'apple' and other things. Then Emma steps through the evening's puddles of light and closes the door.

CHANGING

Henry Wyvern thought it must have been a hell of a party. He felt wretched. His stomach ached and his head was throbbing. His eyes were red and his hair was a mad mop. But that was the test, wasn't it? The worse you were the next day, the better it must have been? He'd never subscribed to that maxim before but he'd never been this sick after a party either. He couldn't remember much of the previous evening. His head pounded as he slowly swung his legs out of bed in order to visit the toilet again. He stopped. The clock showed 3:20 yet it was bright outside. He rummaged for his watch among the strewn clothing on the floor. The time was correct, it was just twelve hours later than he expected. How could he have slept so late?

Henry rang work, making sure he used the office receptionist's number, and made his apologies. Terrible headache. Just woke up. Going back to bed. Should be in tomorrow.

It was better to ring the receptionist at the front desk than his boss. There were fewer questions and no recriminating silences. A glass of water and three headache tablets like rocks to swallow. Henry stood under the shower for half an hour, letting the hot water pelt down on his shoulders and back. His left hand itched. There was a little scratch near his wrist. That girl.

Yes, he'd been dancing and chatting to Sally, the host of the party and secretary of the tennis club. Nice woman, pretty laugh, blonde hair. No chance really of anything happening there though and she wasn't quite his type, he thought, but then who was? Maybe he was being too choosy. Someone had started a new song then that was a bit too fast for him, he thought. Sally went to find someone who would dance to it. Henry decided he would switch to soda water and went to the kitchen. He was reaching into the refrigerator when he bumped into a young woman in a blue dress. Or did she bump into him? Either way, she nicked the back of his hand with a long red fingernail. She said she was terribly sorry. She dabbed at his skin carefully with a wet cloth and made solicitous noises — 'Oh, dear. I do apologise,' and so on. She poured him a glass of wine.

He didn't care about the little accident. He was happy just listening to her, looking at her. He drank some more wine, forgot about the soda water. Long dark hair, rather sinuous figure, her voice, that dress, those red nails — these were the things occupying his mind. When he left the kitchen, he looked through the crowded lounge room but couldn't see her any-where. He approached Sally during a break in the music.

'Sally, do you know who the woman is in a blue dress? Young, dark hair, red nails.'

She frowned. 'No idea. Haven't seen her and that doesn't sound like anyone in the club I know. Maybe she's a friend of a member. Just keep asking around. Ah, Creedence Clearwater! I'm off!'

She melted into the mass of bodies in the centre of the room to dance and Henry continued touring the house, looking for the woman while trying to think how he might strike up a conversation that didn't sound contrived. He gave up after half an hour and going through the place twice. Feeling a little seedy, he called for a taxi to take him home.

The water was banging on to the back of his neck now and the headache wasn't retreating. Henry wiped himself briskly with a towel and slunk back to bed. He slept right through to the following morning and woke feeling bright and well.

The design office was the same as always. Henry was good at his job but seldom inspired by it. As a draftsman there was little chance of being given a really adventurous commission. The firm specialised in residential housing and was known for its traditional styles.

He remembered to ring Sally and thank her for inviting him to her party. Henry casually mentioned the woman in the blue dress but drew a blank again. Sally repeated that she was an unknown, probably a friend of someone who had actually been invited.

He finished the plan for an extension to a large house that was to be built in one of the flashier suburbs and realised that his next project was more or less the same. He wouldn't have objected to living in either place but there was no individuality about them. He wished he could do something special, something that would mark him out as one of a kind. Then he would be noticed.

*

A week later Henry stood brushing his teeth before bed, saw himself in the mirror. He was a bit too pale. Too many hours indoors. He resolved to take a walk each lunch break and get out into the open, feel the sun on his skin.

In the morning he looked even worse. Henry leant closer to the mirror. There was something odd about his skin. The capillaries on his nose and cheeks were quite red, much more visible than they should be. He held up his hands. It was the same there. He felt healthy enough but this was a worry. When a client cancelled an appointment early in the afternoon, Henry took an extended walk through the park near his office. It was good to be outside.

That evening Henry slipped off his socks as he undressed for bed and glanced at his toes. His heart missed a beat. The capillaries were red cotton threads and there was also the distinct blue of the veins. Something else too — something that made him instantly queasy. He moved his feet into the pool of light from the bedside lamp. He could see his muscles. Not just their outline but the colour of his own meat. When he flexed his foot, Henry's stomach churned and he vomited on the carpet, emptying his stomach with four violent spasms. This shocking change was terrible. Ugly. Inexplicable. Entrancing. He was a freak. Within an hour, the skin on his feet became totally transparent. They worked normally but he could see everything inside them — as well as the muscles, veins and arteries that were apparent before, there were tendon sheaths, ligaments, and bones. It left him feeling queasy but he couldn't look away. It was like a science project demonstrating the body at work. The questions jostled. When would it stop? What if it didn't stop? Was there a precedent? Could it be treated? How could he go out anywhere?

Over the next two hours, the rest of Henry began to transform and he couldn't bear to look at any part of himself for long, however much the novelty of it called to him. The condition spread so quickly that before the sun rose, his body was moving about the house in a clear envelope of skin. He drew all the blinds and locked the doors. He cried. He sat down on the lounge and cried. Even in his despair, however, he couldn't resist a brief look in the mirror to see the tears travelling towards his ducts. His lungs swelled and deflated, his intestines quivered like a separate animal living inside him, and he watched it all with an uneasy curiosity. How would any doctor deal with this? If other people had suffered his condition, surely Henry would have heard about it.

Henry could not put off ringing work any longer. He made sure the number he called was at the front desk since he didn't want to speak with any of the management staff or his colleagues. His voice was perfectly normal but he decided to make a few croaking noises.

'Hello, Kristy. It's Henry here. Would you please let the design office know that I'm unwell? I won't be in today.' He remembered to make the last few words sound strained, as if his throat hurt when he spoke.

'Ooh, I hope it's nothing bad. Do you expect you'll be in tomorrow?'

'Well, I'm not sure when I'll be able to return. I just need to rest first. I'll probably be calling tomorrow as well. We'll have to wait and see.'

'I'll tell them. You take care. Sounds like you need some hot water and lemon juice.'

'Thanks, Kristy.'

He hit the red button to end the call. Hot water and lemon juice? Maybe he'd be able to handle that. He certainly had no appetite for food and at first he wouldn't eat even for sustenance. He moped about the house dejected at the idea of seeing his food being digested within him. Eventually the hunger was too much and on the third day he made a light meal of scrambled eggs on toast with a few sprigs of parsley. He forced himself not to look down at his stomach even though it was covered by a dressing gown. The thought of what was going on there appalled him. Worse was looking at his own face in a mirror. It wasn't really a face anymore but a strange multi-layered mask with grotesque eyeballs. He covered the mirrors with alfoil and masking tape, all he could find to do the job.

The food cupboards were running low because he hadn't made his weekly supermarket trip. How could he go shopping in this situation? Henry searched online and found a local store that took grocery orders by phone and also made home deliveries. He ducked out to leave cash under a pot plant on the veranda, careful to check for neighbours.

He couldn't think how he would earn a living if he needed to stay hidden in his own house. On the other hand, it might be possible to make money out of this problem. Someone would pay. A television documentary? No. The public would be curious but horrified and then he would become an outcast. Wasn't he already in self-exile? Why not be a wealthy outcast? Perhaps he could quietly do his design work from home and keep to himself. It might be possible, but then there would inevitably be clients who wanted meetings. All these things whirled in his mind. The first issue, however, was to get help dealing with his condition.

Henry called his doctor's office. 'Could I speak with Doctor Hutchinson, please?'

'When would you like an appointment, sir?'

'Actually, that depends ... on ...' Henry couldn't bring himself to tell her that he could not come into the medical practice. 'Could I just have a brief word with him first.'

'He is quite busy.'

'Just a word?'

'I'll see what he can do. Please hold.'

Henry couldn't think how he might properly spell out his predicament without sounding like he was off his trolley.

'Doctor Hutchinson.'

'Yes, doctor. Thank you. I wanted to know if you have ever treated a condition where a patient's body becomes, well ... where you can kind of see inside, the skin being transparent.'

'I'm sorry, who is this?'

'Henry Wyvern. I'm a regular patient and I didn't want to waste your time making an appointment if what I presented should be taken elsewhere.'

'What did you say it was?'

'My skin is quite transparent and …'

'Ah, skin. That would be dermatology. Not my area, at least as a specialisation. My reception staff could make an appointment for you to see me and I'll look at giving you a referral. I'll transfer you back there now.'

One of the reception desk staff cut in but Henry hung up in frustration. He dithered over whether to call a locum doctor to see him at his home but stopped short of chasing a phone number for one through the online listings. He imagined that whoever turned up to see him would likely have been terrified and done a runner, ready to broadcast the news about this monster. He felt incredibly alone.

Henry became a prisoner in his house, sneaking out in the early hours to clear his letterbox and otherwise hiding inside. His sick leave was almost exhausted when he saw that his skin was changing again, becoming opaque. He feared the possibility of a bizarre new appearance revealing itself, while wishing that he might somehow get his normal body back. It was much quicker this time, taking a little over a day. Small scales began to appear on his shoulders. They looked glossy, as if wet, but were soft and dry, smooth to touch. It was horrible watching them emerge. Henry rang his doctor again and this time blurted out the whole thing as best he could through his sobbing.

'Doctor Hutchinson, I have this terrible skin condition. I need help now.'

'Ah, Henry. I did suggest seeing a dermatologist. If you come in, we can get you a referral for that. I can't do it over the phone.'

Henry ploughed on. 'First it was like my skin was turning to clear plastic, still flexible but I could see through it. Right through, like glass. I could see *everything*. And then it started changing into scales, lizardy things and …'

'Can I just interrupt for a moment, Henry? It sounds like you're stressed.'

'Well, yes, I am. Who wouldn't be? It's tormenting me.'

'I think you need a good rest and some time off work. If you come into the practice, I'll arrange a sick certificate to give your employer and we can talk about your skin worries. Now, I do have to see some other patients.'

Before Henry could respond, Hutchinson hung up on him.

Henry's whole body developed a sleek covering like snakeskin. It revolted him at first; it was even worse than having transparent skin. After a few days, however, he came to appreciate it more. Not having one's inner workings on display had to be an improvement of sorts, though he still couldn't bring himself to go outside. He researched the Internet for clues to his dilemma but there was nothing.

Henry also listed what he had left in his pantry and stretched out the supplies as best he could. He made two orders for home delivery of what might last longest in the cupboard; pasta, canned tomatoes, rice, long-life milk, potatoes, and so on. Cooking itself was not pleasant. It was taking him a while to adjust to his own scaly fingers, because of their slipperiness and also their appearance.

His bank balance was running low. He had only $250 above what he needed to cover rent to the end of the month and $85 in cash in his own apartment. He would have to do something. Henry wrote a letter of resignation from his job. No one had even rung him while he was away. They didn't care about him and the job was dull anyway. The termination pay would last him a few months and give him time to plan. As yet there were no ideas, but he tried to convince himself that something would happen if he applied himself to it. He was creative, after all. Henry propped the letter on the kitchen table. His routine was now to sleep during the day so he went to bed. He intended to slip out during the night wearing an overcoat and his biggest hat so he could drop the resignation into the street-corner post box.

When he woke, he saw that the pattern on his skin was fading. It had been rather elegant, diamond shapes in three shades of coppery brown. Part of him was rather sad to see it going, but only part. What would be next? To his surprise, what was showing underneath the snake-like skin was pinkish and human. He could hardly dare to hope. Henry stayed up all day, frequently checking himself in the mirror, holding out his hands and feet for a sign of something else appearing. With great relief he saw that his skin was looking normal again, just like his old skin but with the bonus that small scars and blemishes were gone.

Two days later, Henry rang his office to say that he had been given the all clear and that his chest cold was no longer infectious. He blinked his way through the brilliant light of day and picked up his design project where he'd left off, but this time with some relish. Henry's life returned to its old routine. His work was predictable and a little boring but he minded that less than before. He even kept up his lunchtime walks through the park. He had missed two weeks of his life. Or rather he had experienced two weeks like no one else. It excited and frightened him. It was a time he could never discuss with anyone. In the following month there was no sign of a relapse so Henry was happy to accept an invitation to a weekend party. It would get him back into the social swing, he thought. He bought a royal purple jacket for the occasion. It was brighter than he would usually have chosen but he was feeling buoyant.

On the night of the party he was deciding between red and blue socks, both pairs spread on his bed. He was already half an hour late. Red would match his jacket. He sat down to pull the red ones on when something made him stop. His chest tightened and his breath wheezed. On his feet was the unmistakeable shape of another pattern emerging. Leopard spots? They looked like leopard spots. Henry threw the socks across the room. He grabbed the bedside lamp and threw that too, smashing against the bedroom door. Henry punched the door and then punched the wall for good measure. He swelled up with anger and let out a howl that shocked him so much he cut it short and slumped onto the bed. He didn't sit for long. Whatever was going to happen now, it would take most of the night for the change to occur. Henry might at least get in a few hours at the party before he would have to leave. It could be the last chance to mix with other human beings for a long time.

The party was going strong when Henry arrived. There were cars jamming the street and parked all over the lawn, the throb of loud music, shouted conversations, dancing. The kitchen sink was awash with empty bottles and melting ice. Henry downed three glasses of brandy in succession. His hands had jittered with anxiety on the way to the party but that slight tremor was fading. The tension in his arms and back was disappearing too. He moved through the crowd and shut himself in the downstairs toilet.

Henry eased one sock down a fraction. There was no sign of new spots appearing higher up, so he walked back into the lounge-room, straight to the heart of the ruckus. He danced with a couple of women and, considering the volume of the music, managed a relatively long conversation with a third. Despite his wish to indulge himself, he began to feel it was all a bit too frenetic.

Henry poured himself another scotch and wandered through the house. One of the back bedrooms was unoccupied. He closed the door behind him, pulled back the curtains and slumped onto the bed. The rear of the house faced a deep gully. Henry lay for a few minutes looking through the window. It was dark out there but for a few small lit windows in houses on the other side. The party was not for him anymore. It was time to leave. He was lifting himself onto one elbow when there was a quick knock on the door.

'Ah, Henry. You're a hard man to find.'

He couldn't take his eyes off her. It was the woman from the previous party, this time dressed in a light golden fabric that floated about her. She wore high boots of creamy leather and her hair fell in a loose sweep across her breasts. It was a '70 movies cliché look but he assumed a deliberate one. She looked at him just a little too long for politeness before glancing away, then sat beside him and briefly patted his leg.

'Sorry about the scratch.'

Henry swallowed. 'That? I'd forgotten ... it was nothing.'

She turned to face him.

'Oh, I wouldn't say that, Henry. Certainly not that. Let me show you something.'

She bent and slid off her boots. 'Turn that bedside light on and tip it this way, would you?'

Henry switched the small light on and angled it towards her. The woman raised a long leg onto the bed beside him and he stared.

'You know about this, don't you?'

Henry's eyes followed the curve of her thigh, the shapely calf, and stopped at her ankle.

'I had to scratch you, Henry. I wanted you. And it gets so lonely.'

The leopard spots on her ankle were just like his. He bent to kiss them.

EASY MONEY

It seemed like a good idea at the time. Not the robbery, which was a good idea all the time — certainly for the whole six months we spent planning it. We had that thing pictured down to the least detail, walked it through until we had it pat; left nothing to chance. No, it was the other thing, afterwards, that changed it all.

One minute you're jogging along the footpath with sixty thousand dollars or so in a bag wedged against your chest — nothing too obvious in that, could have been someone keen to catch a bus. Don't run too fast in case you fall over. Then you're slipping into the getaway car, a nicely inconspicuous Toyota, with Terry sliding behind the wheel on the other side. It didn't stall either — new battery. We'd thought of that. In fact, we had the car serviced the week before and got a tune-up too, just in case, and it started every morning with a lovely little hum. We checked the tyre pressure, stole some plates the night before. It could have been a pensioner's car, someone simply out shopping for groceries, though ski masks aren't that common on pensioners, on a warm day in late spring

The sirens were still a distant and somehow sweet song when Terry eased us out into the roadway and the Aston Martin tore into the driver's door. Jesus, did that make a noise, and a mess, of both cars. If anything, I think the Toyota fared better but even with Terry trying vigorously for a few seconds — backing up, rolling toward the kerb and trying to drive over it, and so on — we were clearly not going to be making any kind of smooth and unobtrusive get-away from that point on. Still, that was not the big problem.

The owner of the Aston started to get out of his crumpled, Nile green fastback. I've always liked that colour; understated, you know. It says 'I'm as wealthy as all hell, but I know when not to flaunt it' — not like Ferrari drivers. Anyway, he had his door open and then he saw the ski masks, I suppose, and he froze. I reckon he was going to stand there with his mouth open and, a few seconds later, slide back into his car as if he had forgotten something, discretion being the better part and all, but the bugger kept on coming. He was walking around the front of the damaged Aston with what looked like a handgun, and he was raising it. In our direction. I call that bad manners; right out of order. Terry saw it too because he piled out of the door on my side of the Toyota, straight over the top of me and giving me an inadvertent kick in the head with his boot as he went. I was right behind him.

Fortunately, the spot where we had decided to stop was on the corner of a public park with some dense shrubbery. Terry and I ploughed through that stuff like bulldozers, heading nowhere except away from Aston man, and as fast as possible. As luck would have it, there was hardly any traffic on the road running down the other side when we emerged. The little that was there was slowing. Maybe Terry chose the Lexus because it was white and bland looking, another Toyota really, though with pretensions. Maybe it was because it was closest. I had to admire the way he simply banged on the roof, raced around and wrenched the driver's door open, then hauled the guy onto the ground. We were away as quick as you can say u-turn.

I don't know whether Aston man would have got there soon enough to see us do it, though there were witnesses who'd have clocked the show. People in other cars, maybe a few pedestrians nearby — and, as I realised a few seconds later, the two others sitting in the back of the Lexus. But it wasn't them who stuffed it all up. They were just a bride and her father on the way to a wedding, and they looked as startled as I felt.

'Terry,' I said, but he was intent on pushing the Lexus through the traffic with the right balance between making time and only speeding a little bit, just that fraction of difference that might not draw too much attention. He's a good driver.

'Terry?'

'What?'

'We have company.'

Terry quickly scanned the road ahead, then glanced in his side mirror and after that the rear view mirror for a sign of any cops.

'Can't see any,' he said, and then, 'Oh, shit!'

His head swivelled like in one of those cheap horror movies, taking in the pair in the back seat for just an instant before swinging back to the road in front of us.

'Bugger!' Then, 'You two! Look away.'

He didn't speak again but carved a slightly faster path towards the next intersection and zigzagged through some side streets that brought us to another but smaller park.

'Out!' he hissed.

The bride looked like she didn't know whether to cry or yell. Her hands gripped the edge of the seat while the old man, her father surely, just quivered and sat grey-faced.

'I said Out!'

Neither of them moved. I instinctively curled my fingers around the bag, though these two were no threat to our haul — just a delay.

The bride slowly leant forward, just a couple of inches. 'Terry …'

'It's not his real name,' I said, realising as the words came out how lame it sounded.

'Just get out, right now!' Terry added.

'I know your voice,' she said, softly. 'There's no point pretending.'

Even through the ski mask I could tell that he was licking his lips, hesitating. 'Who is it then? The groom.'

'Alan Broadbank, from the hardware store. You'd like him. He's not like you, but still, who else is, Terry? He treats me and the boy well.'

'You have to get out. Please.'

'Come on, Dad,' she said, and gathered up the huge folds of her dress. 'Help me out.'

'I'll get her,' I said to Terry. 'You help the old man.'

We were back underway in less than a minute, pulling off our masks this time. It wasn't fair, I was thinking, they should have had ribbons on the front of these cars every time so you could tell. Terry wasn't talking, which isn't that odd for Terry but this was a different kind of not talking. Finally, he started, 'I, er ...'

'No, you can't. Don't even think about it.'

'It's her wedding day, Rory. What kind of bastard would I be if I didn't ... ?'

'I'd say she didn't have that high a regard for you as it was, and this won't have helped. Let it lie. You may have noticed we're in kind of a jam here.'

'Just to wish her well, you know. The decent thing.'

'No!' I said firmly, even as he turned back in the direction of the park. 'We planned this for months.'

'We didn't plan on her.'

'Terry!'

'It won't take long. I can let you out, with the money, if you like. We can meet up later.'

I closed my eyes. 'Make it quick for God's sake.'

They were still there, the old guy sitting on a kid's swing and her hovering protectively like some weird angel. Terry walked over and they spoke, not for long, just a couple of minutes. I switched to the driver's seat, in case, tapping the wheel.

Wouldn't they have phoned someone by now? The cops could be minutes, even seconds away. Where would a bride have kept a mobile phone, though? And the old bloke, maybe he didn't have one. I was about to give the car horn a little toot when Terry came back, breaking into a run.

'We definitely cannot drive her to the wedding!'

'No, it's alright, I let her use my phone. Someone will be here soon.'

'Yeah, the cops.'

'Let's go,' he said. 'There's a hotel up the road. Big car park. We can easily pinch another ride.'

I wasn't letting him off that easily. 'What was that really about?'

He grunted.

The hotel car park was nearly full and we tucked the Lexus in a far corner, away from the road. I was looking at a plain tradesman's van that we might grab for our next transport. Terry's gaze was fixed on a sleek Audi sports in metallic grey, and then on me.

'Do you believe in fate?' he said.

That's when I knew we were stuffed.

'No, Terry,' I said, 'I don't, and this isn't right.'

'We're gone, mate. Might as well enjoy it for what's left'

When he drove the Audi out of there alone and with a cheeky chirruping of the tyres, he could have had a big neon light on its roof saying Nicked. It wasn't going to be long. I went into the pub and had a whisky — double, top shelf — and then another one. I thought about paying for them and leaving a fifty thousand dollar tip, but Terry had taken the money after all. As a favour to me, I suppose. I just pulled out a twenty for the bartender and then went to the bus stop outside. When they came to my flat, Terry was a step behind them, in handcuffs. He shrugged his shoulders.

So. He's still got two years to serve and I'm out on parole, working for a bloke who has a lawn-mowing round. I might get my own some day. It's honest enough work. And fate, whether or not you believe in it, has given me a customer who used to own a Nile green Aston Martin. He doesn't recognise me, which is just as well. The prick has a blood red Ferrari now, and keeps dispensing dodgy business advice. I know he deals drugs on the side, for the thrill, but I keep my mouth shut. Never know when it might come in handy.

So, why did Terry do it? Why had he insisted on going back? I visit him every second week and he told me, eventually. It was to give her a wedding present. I had noticed the pale skin on his finger where a ring had been as we headed for the hotel, but hadn't thought to ask at the time. We were a bit busy then.

'The ring,' I said.

'Nah. I pawned that to get the car tuned. It was to tell her to forget me,' he said. 'I called her names you wouldn't call a dog, to make it clear. You know; break it completely.'

'You said goodbye by going back? I used to think you were pretty bright.'

'Yeah. Look where it got me.'

*

The bride comes to see him on alternate weeks. Her marriage lasted almost a year. Terry says he doesn't know, but he's hopeful.

'You could do worse,' I said. 'Much worse.'

WHOEVER YOU ARE

Wherever I go I have acquired bits of someone else's life. It is someone I suspect I'll never meet. I'm not sure who he or she is. More than one name appears. It changes from one purchase to the next. If this attempt to hide their true identity is out of shame at reduced circumstances or due to an intense paranoia and need for privacy, I may never know.

Today I found another piece of the puzzle. It was a copy of *A Book of English Essays* — including the musings of Bacon, Lamb and a nominally less edible author, Quincey, among others. Inside the cover was a scrawled name which might have been Arthur Kit but the ink was faded and the writing difficult to decipher. The name may just have been a red herring but I paid a dollar for this bit of Kit. A solitary scholar. A bargain.

Think about the dollar. Once we had pennies and ha'pennies and farthings. Then the cents and two-cent pieces that overtook them were snatched up in a corrective sweep. This morning I found myself looking at a five-cent piece that had failed to scratch up the requisite three matching numbers on a lottery ticket and I wondered if its days were also numbered. Why stop there? At the current rate of inflation we may only need five dollar coins or greater before I shuffle off.

Last week my discovery was a slightly watermarked copy of *The Motorcyclist's Workshop.* I knew it was his (or hers) the instant I picked it up, though there was no name inscribed in it. Another of his/her tricks. It was the sought-after 1947 edition with the opening chapter on the ideal workshop. It was just the sort of book I had come to expect — eclectic but not flashy; erudite and specialised. I am not sure whether I like best the line-drawing illustration of that workshop, with its awning windows open and, I imagine, a frosty English morning outside, or the neat figure of the motorcycle enthusiast printed on the cover. The latter, I think. He is posed there carefully hacksawing some small and vulnerable mechanical apparatus that is sensitively held in a bench-vice. There is something tender in his posture, something of the physician, but it is his clothing that I admire more. His sleeves are rolled for work but under the knitted, sleeveless jumper his wife made for him the previous autumn he is still wearing a tie. Even in the garden shed, and in the company of a road-soiled, oily motorcycle, he has not lost his sense of decorum. When I gaze at the cover, I feel I know the last owner of the book very well. It cost me twenty-two dollars, though that's not to say it is twenty two times the value of the copy of *A Book of English Essays* I found for just a dollar.

Who is this person? An enigma wrapped in an enigma, as they say. After all, he or she also recently left a copy of Seamus Heaney's *Door into the Dark* for me to find on a church fundraising-stall. A first edition on a church stall! There is no poem in it titled 'Door into the Dark,' which is clearly part of its charm, though there are plenty of fine words about what light does in various airs and one must concede that Mister Heaney does a fair job of imagining people. That was three dollars, less than a month ago. The scattered placement of these titles is the work of a master. How would it be possible for someone to know in advance where I might be looking at second-hand books? I am no Sherlock Holmes but I think a great mind is at work here.

There could be another explanation for why the former owner of these books is so shy of me, something more than the previously mentioned ones of disgrace or fear. It is that the whole thing is an elaborate game. I don't like to think of someone toying with me in this fashion, however. It's quite unsettling. And apart from the silly assumption of godly authority involved, it is simply out of character, beyond what I have come to know of the man. And you see now that I must drop the he/she equivocation. The person is male.

Whoever he is.

Whoever you are.

There may be other evidence but you can see it is the books that provide me with the best clues. I am more tuned in to them and what they say about this fellow. I know when I discover one that it is another step on the way to knowing what I must know.

I decided to lay a little trap of my own. I selected three titles that I would donate to particular charities. These were all books he had owned. I included Volume 7 of *The Meaning of Modern Art*. It is sub-titled 'The Dominion of the Dream' and I'm sure he would be excited to see it again.

I knew the charities had their sales on different days of the week. That is why I chose them, so I should be able to visit each place in turn and, while pretending to look over the other stock,

I should be able to see who finds and buys the books I have placed there or, at least, lingers for a long time over them. Something would be the key; a briefly startled expression perhaps. Or, as I expect, if I found that I was dealing with a much cooler customer, then I would have to shadow them a while after they leave. I had a notebook and pen and a thermos packed, plus enough change for a bus or train journey provided it is within the bounds of the city.

But there is a nagging thought, even a dilemma, that might leave my plan in disarray. It occurred to me that if the books I have bought did slowly construct an image of the previous owner, then they may also say something of me. What if it was not the previous owner who reclaimed the books? What if someone new bought them? Somewhere out there would be the next owner, waiting to find me out.

I decide I must abandon my plan. It gives me a peculiar feeling to be so circumscribed, so hemmed in. I realise now that when the time comes for me to dispose of my books, I will have to be very careful. Just to think of leaving them all is a source of heartache, but one day I must. I cannot bear to think of destroying them. I will have to be sure to spread them widely; one book in this jumble sale, a couple given to that charity, another to a church fete, and so on. It will be laborious but essential work. You never know who is out there, watching.

BEFORE IT ALL FELL APART

'Let me do the talking.'

'Why?'

'Because I'll know what to say.'

'Jesus, Frank. You can be such a ...'

'Shut up, here he comes.'

The cop hitched his belt as he drew level with the driver's door. He made a show of flipping a notebook open with one hand and holding a pen just above it.

'Okay, folks. In a bit of a hurry?'

'How can I help you, officer?' Frank smiled.

'Do you know how fast you were going back there?'

'Well, not speeding, that's for sure.'

The cop paused for a second. 'Say, aren't you ... ? Well, I'll be! Wait until I tell the boys back at ...' He squinted and checked himself. 'Tell me now, which way did you folks come?'

Frank smiled and turned to Ava. 'It was down through Seven Lakes, wasn't it, honey?' He faced the policeman again, 'Yeah, that was it.'

'Is there a problem, officer?' said Ava. Frank pinched her leg without taking his friendly gaze off the cop. Ava knew what that meant and bit her lip.

'The cop tipped his hat back a little, a gesture somewhere between uncertainty and remembered manners for the beautiful dark-haired passenger.

'Well, Miss Gardner, there could be. We've had reports of vandals, some destruction of property. Car like this, too, with its fancy paint and them wheels and all. Don't see so many of these about.' He scanned the length of it for an instant. 'Not in Indio. Even with Hollywood up the road.'

Ava glanced at Frank, who maintained his calm regard of the policeman.

'I hate to get too official, Mr. Sinatra, but right now I do need to see a driver's licence.'

'Well, Officer, er ...'

'Kowalski.'

'Officer Kowalski. I'm sure I can oblige but my licence is somewhere in a bag inside the trunk. Might take some hunting around.'

'Mmmm. Well, I s'pose I don't want you folks having to unpack everything on the side of the road and all. Tell you what, the station is just down the way, and we can sort this out there. You know, out of sight of the public.'

Ava thought of reaching into the glove box while the cop was distracted talking. Frank's licence was there; she'd seen it when he opened it a few minutes earlier and pulled out the two .38s. Before the shooting began. Such a lousy shot, he was. But then she was too. Anyway, if she quickly slipped the licence out and passed it to Frank, they might be able to get on their way without a fuss. But there was also the last of the whisky bottle in there too and the cop's attention flitted back and forth now as if he was afraid to miss anything. It was too risky, she decided.

Frank patted her on the thigh. 'Sounds fine, officer. Shall we follow you?'

Ava and Frank sat in the front office of the police station while Kowalski wrote down the details of Frank's licence. A gawping assistant hovered nearby, fidgeting at his tie and pistol belt while sneaking looks at Ava's legs.

When the two policemen quietly conferred, Ava leant over to Frank. 'What if they search the car? They're going to find the guns, Frank! I told you we should have ditched them on the way here.'

'No. They'd be found soon enough and then it'd be worse, right? They're just for self-protection, anyway. Who doesn't have a gun ... or two. Listen, you just keep your mouth shut about them, okay? And if we're asked, you still keep it shut. Nothing.'

'I'm not as dumb as you seem to think, Frank.'

Kowalski approached and moved to hand back Frank's licence, then stopped, shaking his head just the once. 'Mr. Sinatra, I have to ask you this. Would you mind if we had a look in the car?'

Sinatra's demeanour changed instantly. He stood up from the bench seat and scowled. 'You can do that, Kow ... Officer Kowalski. But you know, I would strongly suggest that you wait until my attorney gets here.' He glared straight into Kowalski's eyes.

'Well, I suppose that's what we could do, Mr. Sinatra. You could phone him. And then we could all have a little talk about the shot-out streetlights, and several shop windows, a coupla street signs too. That would be just about when you folks were driving through. Two o'clock in the morning. Maybe you saw something, being there at the time and all.'

'I gotta make a call, officer. And you know I'm allowed.'

'How long do you think it would take for your attorney to get here, Mr. Sinatra?'

'Why?'

Ava interrupted. 'Officer, I have a rehearsal at the studio at ten.' There was the faintest coo in her drawl. 'Do you think we might get there in time?'

'Miss Gardner, that all depends.'

'I want my call,' Frank barked.

Kowalski turned to his partner. 'Bobby, please take Mr. Sinatra into my office. He can call from there.'

As soon as Frank left, Ava gave Kowalski a slow smile. 'I reckon I know your accent, Officer. Carolina or thereabouts, no?'

'Greenville.'

'See. Me, I was born in ...

'Grabtown, North Carolina. I read the motion picture papers sometimes.'

'Well, I am flattered. It was Smithfield, actually. Not far from your Greenville.'

'I hope you weren't involved in this shooting activity, Miss Gardner. You two wouldn't have been drinking, would you?'

Ava crossed her legs slowly. 'I don't know what you mean, I'm sure. Now I wonder if Frank, Mr. Sinatra, has finished his call.' She tipped her head towards the adjacent office and the animated silhouette just discernible through its frosted window.

'I only asked about the attorney,' Kowalski continued, 'because it would be a shame if there were … if there were reporters here before we concluded our business, that's all. Been known to happen.'

Ava frowned. 'You'd better take that up with Frank, officer.'

Frank walked out of the adjacent room with a grin. 'It's okay, honey. Appears they know it was somebody else now. It's fine. Officer, your captain is on the line. Anytime you're in Hollywood, let the studio know; you can have a private tour of the place. I appreciate you were doing your job. Come on, Ava, let's go.'

It took Kowalski a moment to absorb the fact that his big stars were leaving, without a search of the car and without an attorney actually visiting.

Frank took Ava's arm. 'Nothing else we need to do here, Ava. Let's go.'

'But Mr. Sinatra …' Officer Kowalski stuttered.

Sinatra did not stop. 'Straight out the door and get in the car,' he murmured to Ava, then added over his shoulder, 'Talk to your boss, Officer Kowalski. Nice to meet you.'

Frank drove directly towards Palm Springs and home. At first his jaw was set and he stared straight ahead, keeping his thoughts to himself. He gradually began to relax, his hands loosening a little on the wheel.

'Frank, was that really his boss on the phone?'

'I truly hope so. Ava, you really have to learn to keep that sweet mouth shut. You let me take care of things and they turn out okay, right?'

There was a sign for a diner ahead and he pulled the car over to the side of the road. 'You know, I really could do with something to eat. How about you?'

'Yeah, I guess. But this place is closed.'

Frank checked. The outside lights were on but it was dark inside. He leaned across the car, deliberately grazing Ava's left breast as he reached into the glove box. He retrieved one of the pistols. 'One last go. You can have a shot too if you want.'

'No, thank you.'

Frank levelled the .38 at the front of the diner and squeezed the trigger. A large window shattered into a momentary dazzle of shards. He slipped the gun away and floored the accelerator. 'Let them try pinning that one on Frank Sinatra. Dumb sons of bitches.'

'Let's go home now, Frank.'

'Don't you want some more fun?'

'I want some sleep before I get to the studio.'

'Fucking studio!' Frank clenched the wheel.

'Don't worry, honey. The studio couldn't drop you just like that. They'd regret it when another one grabs you from right under their noses.'

'Well, you go to bed and get your damned beauty sleep. I know where there's a game and I'm going.'

'Take me home and then you can catch a cab.'

'It's not like it was much of a town, really. All we did was ruffle a feather or two.'

'I grew up in a place a bit like that, Frank.'

'All the more reason to take some shots at it.'

Ava watched as the cab turned out of the driveway but Frank didn't wave or acknowledge her standing out there watching him leave. She walked down to Frank's prized Chrysler. She could never figure why he liked them so much when he could have had any fancy make, a Cadillac or something. He had left the guns in the glove box and she took one.

Her first shot punctured the passenger door simply because that was the closest. To balance things out, she walked around and shot the driver's side door as well, then buried a bullet in the radiator and another in a headlight. She shot the Chrysler symbol on the hood for good luck. And just one more, she thought.

Standing in front of the car, its paintwork gleaming in the light from the front porch of the house, she aimed at the obvious target. The windshield exploded into thousands of pieces. Enough. Time for bed.

BURNT OFFERINGS

Patrick was eating late, as usual. At least, he was trying to eat — past midnight and part way through another meal for one. Any meal for one seemed like half a proper meal since Gemma had left. There should be two plates, he thought, staring down at the table; two sets of cutlery.

Though he was good at cooking it was now simply routine, necessary but dull. He carried out the ritual mechanically, as one might brush teeth. Gather the ingredients, follow the steps in preparation, set the table, eat, and wash up. All performed robotically but without enough attention, often getting the proportions of the ingredients wrong or burning the food. Worse was standing at the kitchen bench with vegetables or a cup of rice in hand and suddenly remembering a particular dish they used to enjoy together. That was always good for a few minutes of maudlin reflection. Unhealthy nostalgia, he told himself, useless stirring of old memories. Get over it.

But he continued to defer meals or to skip them altogether. This night he poked a knife at a largely untouched and somewhat singed omelette, then pushed the plate away, rested his chin on his hands. It was far too late to be eating, anyway. And she was gone, gone, permanently gone. You might as well do it now, he thought. Get over it? Yes. Get it over with. Patrick slid his chair back and left the table.

He spilled the letters onto his bed in a wide arc of coloured envelopes and sheets of the ivory writing paper she had liked so much. Paper he had spent ages searching for in shops across the city, trying to get exactly what she had wanted. There was no longer any point pretending that putting the letters in a seldom-used drawer or tucking them high up in a cupboard would work. They might lie forgotten for a while, but he would always go back to them eventually. The scent, the feel of the paper, the words she had scrawled across the pages; their presence would pull him in like spells. It was the same cycle over and over; the constant temptation and self-recrimination, then his surrender and wallowing in all the outdated details of her writing, the physicality of the envelopes and paper, before he decided on another storage place. He was running out of those.

It would have to be a quick and complete cut. The rubbish bin? Appealing, but impractical. It was three days until the next rubbish collection. He would not be able to stop thinking about Gemma's letters lying out there. That wouldn't be throwing them out. Not really. More like torture. It would have to be total destruction. Something irreversible, like … yes … burning. There was no other way. He would not open even one, no last looks. He placed his hands across the fan of paper on his bed for a moment, then swept it into a fat bundle and went looking for matches.

There was no open fireplace in his flat. Patrick took the letters out to the small rectangle of lawn in front of the apartment block. The grass was wet. Matches spluttered and fizzed and the crumpled newspaper he stuffed around the letters produced a brief flutter of yellow flames that soon died. He scuffed at the lawn with his heel, trying to get the moist grass out of the way but it always ended the same.

The street light on the corner hummed. Its sodium glare sank through the trees and coated him in its sickly glow. He looked up at the light through the foliage. Okay then. The road. That would be dry enough.

Patrick stacked the letters in a tepee shape on the edge of the dry roadway, almost in the gutter. He'd once seen a sketch of a campfire arranged that way so the air would be sucked up through the middle and get things burning properly. He struck a match. Its small light was almost friendly in the middle of the rough pyramid of paper. Nothing. Then a flicker; something caught and licked around the base of an envelope. He recognised that one. She had been on a conference trip to Queensland and wrote of her boredom there, her urgent need to hold him again. She hadn't mentioned the sales manager in her room every night. Burn. Fry. Twist, you little fucker. Every night. Lunging over her, tasting her, making her squeal. The next letter flashed alight. That was the one she sent from her holiday in New Zealand. Next time, Patrick, you should come too, she wrote. I'll be able to show you the best spots. The steaming pools she had seen; the sulphurous air she had smelt; the carvings in the Maori lodges. Not a word about the nights though. Nothing about the German eco-tourist she met. Was there one? A linguist perhaps? A researcher, or a journalist? Some interloper she invited closer with the practised shyness of her brief downward glance.

He was aware of a movement behind him. It was past one in the morning now and no one else should have been awake but there was definitely someone there. He looked over his shoulder. It was the woman from the flat above, her gown pulled tight against the cold. In three years he had only ever nodded a hello to her on the stairs.

'Rubbish,' he explained. 'Getting rid of some rubbish,' and pushed a straggling strip of blue ribbon into the flames. All the dumb, festive colours. Another envelope collapsed in a soft explosion of sparks.

His visitor did not speak but retreated across the lawn towards the block of flats, her thin gown waving in the winter air.

When Gemma went, she hadn't left even a note. Strange after all her letters, her endearments, her fondness of explanation. She hadn't rung him either. She was there when he went to work one morning and not there when he came home. He fretted the night away, and rang her office the following day but she had quit work and left no details. The girl closest to being her friend said she thought Gemma might have gone back to England. What did he know about Gemma? What was there apart from these flimsy bits and pieces, her affectionate declarations in expansive swirls and swoops? A whirlwind courtship, a registry wedding and these letters, now giving themselves up in a series of little gasps.

Something fell past his shoulder and into the fire. He glanced up. The woman from upstairs was back, in her hand a fat brick of photographs.

'Bastard,' she said, softly, and dropped another one past him.

Patrick glimpsed a man with short hair in one of them, a bright blue jumper and a big smile. His arm was around a woman's shoulders but she too was swallowed quickly in flame.

'Bastard.'

Another photograph.

'Bastard,' each one.

Patrick poked at Gemma's letters, almost burning his fingers, and laid another one in the fire, then stood up and looked his neighbour in the eyes. Neither spoke. Patrick walked back to his flat. There was one more thing he wanted.

A third person stood at the fire when he returned, with something held tightly to his chest. He recognised Mikal Vella from the house on the opposite corner, wearing an old raincoat over striped pyjamas. The fire had grown. Some magazines were rolling their pages in the heat, the colour pictures turning into negatives of lustrous black and green like rooster's feathers before crumbling, feeding the spiral of ash that puffed into the air.

'Gone,' Vella said. 'She's gone.'

Patrick twisted the silk shirt in his hands a moment longer then added its sheer fabric to the fire. He had found it in the drawer the day after she flew out. But why this? Why had she left only this? Because he'd bought it for her? A crackle and rush of hot air. The three of them squinted at the smoke and heat. As they stepped back, an arm reached through and thrust a small red box, its lid inlaid with mother-of-pearl, into the fire. The glossy shell-work fractured and arched. The thin wooden lid curved and split into long blackening splinters. For a second something papery was visible, tied with wide ribbons that charred and crisped. Someone else's old love letters? A section of heavy timber shelving appeared over Patrick's shoulders and was dropped onto the fire, crushing the remains of the box.

Vella began crying. The woman from the flat above Patrick was just behind him now and he heard her begin to cry also, all stifled whimpers and sniffing. More neighbours were arriving. The faces of the newest ones were wet with tears. All shared a slow, oddly private weeping.

A man emerged from the garden of the house alongside the apartments, awkwardly carrying a chair. They parted to let him through. With eyes brimming he tipped the chair into the fire.

'Made it for her.'

He stood off at a small distance, watching the fire consume it, his knuckles pushed against his mouth. Others passed him, strange pilgrims with their offerings. Patrick recognised a few faces; the owner of the corner shop, the retired mechanic from the end of the block of flats, a teacher who lived in the next street. There were many he could not place; more and more of them, each bearing their own thin combustible or solid slow-to-ignite objects. The bringers stood in a ragged and widening circle, watching in an oddly solitary, communal grief. All the time the occasional slow incantation of 'Bastard' floated over them. And still more people came, carrying their awful parcels.

A blue light swam across the end of the road and a police car idled up to the edge of the crowd. A lanky cop unbent from the driver's side and walked over to the fire. He looked solemnly at the faces around him, then reached into his jacket and withdrew a wallet, slipped out a photograph and let it sail down. He retreated to the patrol car, leant his arms on its roof and sank his head onto them. The blue light continued its lazy rotation. Meanwhile, the fire grew larger, its little red stars rising into the black night air. Patrick watched them on their haphazard journey into the darkness above his suburb.

The fire engine was too late to save the shed on the corner when it burst into flames, and the brush-fence in front of Vella's house took only seconds to collapse in a wild scatter of sparks. There was the smell of spilt petrol and another fire in a house across the road. The crowd made no move to quell the flames.

Patrick sat in his apartment as first light fell weakly into the room. The street was empty and quiet again. He felt very tired but had been unable to sleep. When the telephone rang, he rose from his couch and picked it up with a curious feeling of lightness. It was an odd time for anyone to be trying to reach him. He waited for the end of the beeps that indicated an overseas call.

'Patrick,' he said.

He knew the other voice when it came. He waited for two or three sentences then put the phone down, letting her continue to speak but without listening. He rubbed his hands through his hair. It smelt of smoke from the remains of the house across the road. He turned his hands over. They were dark with ash. His clothes stank too.

She was still talking when he lifted the phone.

'I'm very hungry,' he said, and cut off the call.

Patrick opened his refrigerator door, hardly registering the cold air that spilled across his legs. Steak with green pepper sauce? An apple pie? There were the ingredients for both. It was time to cook a decent meal, and do it properly.

TIMES TABLES

One time I thought I saw him, at an airport. There was a figure ahead in the crowd, and a chill ran through me like someone had slipped a thin blade of ice between my ribs. One short intake of breath, and I froze. I told myself it was not possible. It couldn't be him; there would be no sense in it. Then he turned his head and I saw a younger, more innocent face. A stranger. The chill subsided. I leant on a nearby row of seats and watched him walk away.

A two-timer. I didn't want to think it, in the beginning, or ever, but that's how things were. Deceit is hard to reckon with, and I should know; I'm a black belt exponent. But I know now I was only fooling myself, thinking that it would be okay some day and he would change his ways.

Three times I told him that was it, all over. Me and the packed bags standing at the door, waiting, and wanting him to think I wasn't waiting, that I would be out of there and walking out of his life the next instant. Down the street already. And he stood too ... on his pride, and wouldn't come for me. Obstinately fiddling with some project in the shed or stuck in front of a TV sports show and not acknowledging me while I stared at my bags on the step. I took them back into the bedroom and set to cleaning or sobbing or both. There will be a time for leaving, I thought, if he doesn't get this right. If *we* can't.

Four times I counted out the days, trying to stay away from the calendar, and knowing it was up there on the damned wall watching me. Four times I made it through the first weeks, enough to get hopeful before the gripping pain and the bleeding and Christ I can't go through this not again don't make me it's not fair can't I just once have it please no. But what's fair got to do with it? That's what I learnt. Hope hasn't got a chance. And that way of making it right wasn't right, really. Who'd want to have a kid to patch over the holes? My body was refusing that option anyway.

Five times he sat on the couch or the edge of the bed or in the car and slumped into a pitiful but resentful shadow of someone I had married. He was acting the hurt side a bit, and he knew I saw that — though there was some genuine regret in him too, I guess. I think he sometimes really did want it better; thought he might change. It never lasted long. What was I to do but punch him, and yell inside where no one can hear and the sound goes down for miles? There were moments when he was sweet, I would remind myself, when he knew how to make me feel desirable and special. But there were the shadows, the women. I went to look at one of them, not that she knew. There was a new girl at his work and it wasn't hard to do the sums. She was at a table with him in his regular haunt, the side bar at the hotel near his office. Big girl, not like me, and maybe ten years younger. All that life in her. Big figure and a summer dress with just enough cleavage to make you want to quiver her breasts a bit, which she did for him when she laughed. And him telling jokes, of course. He did that well.

Six tattoos. Not for anniversaries but for the times he gave me flowers. I went and got a new one then, even if all he gave me was a bunch of sorrows for his remorse, so I had a row of these pretty pictures going partway around my left ankle. Nothing tarty, just little ones, and they were roses, always roses. I imagined one day they would circle me, and that would mean something, though I didn't know what. It would have to become clear when that happened.

Seven times he thumped me so bad I copped bruises I had to hide, even a broken nose, and he was so apologetic the next day. How could I, he would say. That's not me, I'm so sorry. Let's get it behind us and have a holiday, get away, make a fresh start. But friends had stopped visiting, stopped remarking on the cuts or bruises, or stopped trying not to. It was just us two now and no one else. I looked at my bruises and wanted them to fade. Maybe he was right. How could I, I asked myself. It was down to me, and I had to change.

Eight times he was actually unfaithful, not just the five he thought I knew about. These were the long-term things, not the one-night stands. He imagined the little flings didn't count, I suppose. I'm not saying he flaunted them. His callousness didn't extend to that. There was something like discretion in his manner, as if he were protecting me with his silence. Some kind of honour maybe. I didn't thank him for it. The agony columns all say don't blab, don't confess and expect forgiveness. Would I have best stayed in the dark altogether, without him looking to confess? I knew too much.

Nine times, they say it was, but I thought fewer. I don't remember them all. Apparently, there was also one to his left eye I had forgotten about. Some of the stab wounds were superficial but that was because he was struggling across the kitchen floor and making it hard. Just a peeling knife, and you wouldn't think it could go so deep. Poor, beautiful beast. I looked on it as a kindness to us both, really. He didn't want to live. I could tell, and I didn't want to live like that anymore.

Ten times three hundred and sixty five days in prison. That's my nominal sentence. But there were the months when I was awaiting trial, and the concession for good behavior while I was inside, so I was released before term, out in the real world. Then again, out is just a way of saying you have to think it and feel it all over again more vividly, where people are moving around with their normal lives, sharing, and being kind or ugly to each other, while you're just a blank, a zero.

He's still there, in the streets, and airports, and shops, and in my head but I will find someone who isn't him one day. I tell myself that. Time after time.

TAKING THE CAKE

James drummed his fingers on the steering wheel. There was no parking to be found anywhere along King William Road, and he was already five minutes late. A middle-aged blonde in a blue silk scarf and designer sunglasses had just slid her convertible into the only space he had seen, giving him a cheery wave of condolence.

Never mind, today was a day for pleasure, a day for success. He recited his mantra: Mimi, Mimi, Mimi. And then it appeared; a florist's delivery van pulled out from the kerb right in front of him and James swung his Alfa into the vacated spot. Now he could make up the lost time. He left his car and walked briskly towards the bistro on the corner. A quick call to the office on his mobile as he went.

'Tricia, it's James. I'll be at lunch with a client until ... two. No messages, okay? Unless it's about the Atchison deal, of course. Okay? Bye!' What they don't know won't hurt them, he thought. Besides, he was to be a junior partner any day now. It was in the bag.

He checked his watch. Fifteen minutes to fix the surprise for Mimi then, say, an hour for lunch with her, pick up Atchison at two thirty and show him the new apartments project, take him back to the office, a bit of smooth talking and Mr. A. would be signing on the line before the day was out. Perfect end to the week. Life was good!

James stepped into The Blue Hat, Mimi's favourite bistro. It was already beginning to bustle with the lunch trade, the suits and frocks. James spotted the owner at a customer's table and tugged her sleeve. She looked up, distracted.

'Hi!' he beamed. 'James Chalmers, for one o'clock. It's the corner table.' The one by the window, where he had proposed to Mimi.

'Ah, one o'clock? Let's see. Chalmers, yes, you're at the window.'

'Fantastic. Back soon.'

One more stop before Mimi arrived. Everything was falling into place.

Mimi. How was he to have known when he first saw her standing outside his office that she was the boss's daughter? James had been married once before, for two years, and had vowed never to do it again. But that notion was gone in an instant when he met Mimi; he knew immediately that she was *the one*.

It was funny how they had also known the minute they saw it that the cake in the window was *the* cake. They had been returning to their cars after a late-night coffee and paused for a kiss. As they were about to resume their walk, they had seen it in the window next to them — four tiers of iced ivory perfection gleaming in a soft light. Their cake. James wasn't exactly sure what it was that made this cake the only one Mimi would settle for, but there was no doubting her passion for it. And now Mimi had no idea that he had put a deposit on it. She would be so impressed. Today he would pay the balance and bring her back after lunch to show off.

There was no-one in the front of the shop. James coughed and rang the little bell on the counter. A woman entered from the rear kitchen, wiping her hands on an apron.

'Sorry,' she smiled. 'Short-staffed today. I'm covering back and front. What can I do for you?'

'I've come to pay the balance on the wedding cake for Chalmers. It's the big one in ivory; cascade of roses.' James put his receipt on the counter.

The assistant read it slowly, and gave him a look of sympathy that made him suddenly uneasy. 'Ah, Mr. Chalmers. I'm sorry, Mr. Chalmers, but it was damaged. An accident.'

James willed himself to remain calm. He had promised Mimi there would be something special today and there damned well would be.

'Well, okay ... I suppose you'd better just fix it then.' He tried to convey the strength of his will in a gaze that was friendly but firm. 'It *can* be fixed?' He nodded, urging her to agree.

'I'm sorry but it can't be done.'

'I'm sure with some icing and all that, it won't be noticed. It's just a cake.'

'No. It was quite a smash.'

This wasn't what he wanted to hear. 'Look, she ... my fiancée had her heart set on that design. It's exactly what she wanted. If it's a matter of money, I'll pay.'

'We had to destroy it.'

We had to destroy it? She made it sound like a horse. Jesus, thought James. Right, stay calm. 'Well ... okay then, make us another one.'

'I'm sorry, Sir, but our cakes are unique. We never duplicate them; it's a policy.'

'But it's been destroyed, suffered some catastrophic event. It's a non-cake.' He felt as if he was trapped in a Monty Python sketch. 'If you make another one that will be unique too, won't it? It's bound to differ in some tiny way. It will be the only one.'

The woman leant her hands on the counter so that her arms stiffened and she shook her head.

James leant forward too. He spoke softly and slowly. 'Get it back. It's mine.'

'I have another very nice cake that you'll really like. I'm sure your fiancée will adore it. Here.'

The woman left the counter and moved over to a display stand in the window where a ziggurat of jagged icing sheets towered over them. 'See, it's also a four tier and it has these lovely wreaths of ...'

'No.'

'Look, in view of the trouble, I could knock 10 per cent off the price. But you'll need to settle on it now.'

'No.'

'I'll even deliver it.'

'I want you to deliver the cake I paid for.'

'Well, to be fair, you must admit you only paid a deposit, and each order is subject to availability.' She turned over James's receipt and pointed to a mass of incredibly small print.

'It's all in our terms and conditions. And we can't deliver the one you ordered now, it's gone.'

'Gone? I thought you said it was destroyed.'

'Same thing. It was damaged and it will be destroyed. We can't have broken and second-rate goods going out of this shop. We're professionals, after all.'

'So, it's still here then.'

'I didn't say that.'

'You mean you *won't* say.'

'I'm not selling a damaged cake. We have our reputation to consider.'

The door opened as another customer entered. 'Please think over my offer while I see to this gentleman. Now, if you'll excuse me just a minute ...'

She left him standing by the giant fractured iceberg he had just rejected. It was imposing but it was a completely different style of cake. He had promised Mimi a surprise, but not this one. James checked his watch. His appointment with Mimi was in five minutes and she was not a woman to be late. She would be at The Blue Hat any moment and watching for his arrival. He had no time for all this stuffing around.

The woman walked into the rear of the shop and emerged carrying a large pink concoction on a tray. It looked like something for a kids' party, but really expensive. Still, those two things went together in this neighbourhood. The other customer held the front door of the shop open for her.

'I'll just be a second, Mr. Chalmers. When I've helped get this into the Folkestones' car, we'll sort out your order, okay?'

James stared at the cake in the window. He gave it a short angry punch of frustration, and it broke like an ice floe on one of those tedious documentaries about the Antarctic. His hand went right through the flimsy outer layer and stuck firm. He tugged but his watch had snagged on something; his hand wouldn't come out. He tried turning his wrist sharply to each side, hoping that whatever had caught on his watchband might disengage and let him withdraw his hand unnoticed. It just hurt his wrist.

He looked up to see a man on the footpath outside had been watching him through the window. How long had he been there? James smiled politely and wrenched his hand free. The base of the cake was simply icing plastered over a platform of cardboard, wire and some sort of filler. Inedible. No wonder it had snared him. There was a raw pink line on his wrist that stung.

He remembered sliding his fingers around the curve of his mother's mixing bowls when he was a child. The sweet delight of sticky fingers. There had been something naughty about it, even if he had been permitted the indulgence. James shook the thought from his mind and brushed broken icing from his sleeve. Well, definitely not this cake, he decided. As he turned back to the counter, he saw something unexpected. Through the doorway that led to the work area in the rear of the shop, he could see a bench. Sitting on it was a cake that looked exactly like the one he had ordered.

He glanced out into the street and saw his recent spectator was gone. The shop assistant was some distance away, her bottom poking out of the rear door of the Folkestone BMW as she secured their birthday cake. James darted into the rear of the shop.

It *was* his cake! It had to be. They only made one-offs; she had said so herself. He circled it quickly, checking for signs of damage. There was nothing wrong with it at all. The bitch! She'd obviously bumped him for someone who'd offered more money. Did she think he wouldn't guess? Okay, okay. What now? Think quickly, James. He could see the side-alley through a screen-door. Right, no one fucks with James Chalmers! He pulled out the envelope with the rest of the cake money and dropped it on the counter. His cake, no damage, money paid — a done deal.

It was heavier than he had expected. He had to lean it against his chest as he pushed the door open with his foot and stepped out into the alley. Walking with it, if you could call it that, meant looking around the cake periodically and down to one side to get a sense of where he was going. He had to make speed, though, and get some distance between himself and the cake shop before she came searching. With any luck, even when she discovered the loss, being short-staffed might mean she would have to stop to lock up first.

James emerged onto the main footpath, nearly bowling over an Unley matron in the process. She exploded with a loud, *'Really!'* and huffed away.

His car. If he could get the cake safely into his Alfa, he might still get to The Blue Hat in reasonable time. The cake was becoming more difficult to carry. It grew heavier and his arms strained. He chanced a moment to lean against a post and re-balance his load. The top tier was out of kilter but he managed to brace it under his chin. One of the pillars was sinking into the icing. James pushed himself away from the post, carefully glancing back toward the cake shop for any sign of pursuit but there was none, so far.

The cake shed a little rose of icing as he walked on. It shattered on the path and fell into the gutter. No way to stop for it. Can't bend down. Keep focussed on the car. Get to the car.

The cake began to bow increasingly as James lugged it along the footpath. He needed to rest somewhere. He retreated slowly, backwards, into the doorway of a clothing shop, trying to move out of the line of sight of anyone who might be following. He would hardly be able to sprint away. He needed a new strategy but he couldn't think of anything. In the meantime, he rested his back on the window.

Move, move. He shrugged his arms further around the base to get a better hold, curved his shoulders inward to brace the upper tiers, and stepped back onto the path. All things considered there hadn't been too much wear and tear on the journey. There was icing all down the front of his jacket, yes. Some had also come off the decorative ring on the top and smeared his chin. No matter. Smooth out the rough bits with a knife. Dry-clean the jacket. His legs, though, were leaden and his hands slippery with sweat or something else oozing from the chocolatey surface of the cake, but he was going to make it. He could see his red Alfa just a block ahead. Get the cake into the car, tidy up a bit and duck across the road to The Blue Hat. Nearly there.

The second highest tier began to slide. James instinctively ducked his head so he could hold his cheek against the side of it.

He felt exhausted. He told himself to count his steps. Break a job into small achievable chunks and tick off one part at a time. That way just about anything could be done.

Finally, he was there. The cake hadn't suffered any further, though he was walking like Quasimodo on dope — a very tired Quasimodo. He pushed up against the passenger door of his car and sighed. He even allowed himself the pleasure of closing his eyes a moment, still clinging to the cake. It was while he was in that state that it occurred to him — he didn't know how he would open the car door. His shoulders lost strength. To have made it this far ...

James stiffened, bracing himself. He turned slowly and began to lift the cake onto the roof of the coupé. His knees trembled with the weight and it was clear that the structure would not hold. He lowered the cake again carefully, tipping it back slightly against his chest for security, then tried moving forward just far enough to place the edge of the base on the bonnet of the car instead. He balanced it with his left hand while reaching for the door handle with his right. Please don't be locked.

It wasn't. The door began to open, and the cake began to teeter. James froze. If there was a passer-by, he could ask for help. This woman?

'Excuse me ...'

But she stared straight ahead. He thought he even heard her sniff at him as she passed. He was about to abuse her when his mobile phone rang. Mimi? She was ringing to find out where he was. No, a bit soon for that. Jesus, the apartment deal! Four million dollars riding on the afternoon and Atchison chooses that moment to call.

There was no other way. James hauled back on the door savagely and simultaneously lunged to save the cake. The whole thing undulated for a moment and he could see a catastrophe coming but then its movement subsided. The phone kept ringing but at least the door was now open. James hooked one foot under the floor-mounted lever that would allow him to slide the seat back and make room for the cake. Jesus, he thought, you'd want a photo of this; me standing with one foot in King William Road while balancing a four-tier wedding cake. Not likely to happen again. The phone stopped ringing. Now he had his foot under the lever but couldn't work out how to actually push the seat back at the same time. He would have to put the cake in the seat as it was.

The phone rang again. James knelt down and slid the cake through the doorway. The top tier caught on the roof of the car, the second tier caught on the seat belt, the third tier caught on the edge of the seat, and the bottom section capsized in his hands. The whole ragged heap slumped into the passenger seat, a three thousand dollar wreck of white chocolate, cream and sponge filling.

James pulled his mobile phone from his jacket just as it stopped ringing again. He tore his jacket off and threw it into the car, slammed the door shut, and punched up his work number.

'Trish, what? That was you, wasn't it?' He wiped his sleeve across his cheek.

'You don't need to be so gruff with me, James.'

'Just tell me, will you?'

'No, it wasn't me. I think you'll find it was Mr. Parker. He's joining you and Mimi for lunch and couldn't find you.'

James sagged. 'It's all right, Tricia. I see him coming now.' He hit the off button, tucked his phone away, and gave the approaching pair a little wave. Mimi was bubbly, her arm tucked into her father's.

'James, James! You'll never guess. It's so wonderful!'

'Mr. Parker.' James nodded at his boss and future father-in-law, and tried to position himself to block any view into his car.

'Hello, James.'

Mimi pecked a kiss on James's cheek. 'What's that on your chin?'

'Nothing.' James whisked his hand across the offending bit of cream. Mimi didn't see that. Anyway, she had something else on her mind.

'Daddy is such a sweetie. You know that wedding cake we really liked? Well, Daddy has done something amazing. When I told him about it yesterday, he went straight to the shop and bought it. It's his present to us.'

James's legs trembled. He propped himself on the Alfa.

'Well, I knew it meant so much to my girl,' said Mimi's father, and gave her a hug. 'Someone else had put a deposit on it but I made what I would call an irresistible offer. Paid an extra thousand.'

'Oh. Good.'

'James? Are you feeling okay?' Mimi squeezed his hand.

'We can share lunch,' Mr. Parker continued. 'Mimi's taking my car back home afterwards, so we can pick up Atchison in your little runabout together. Okay, James?'

James managed a kind of smile. 'Actually, I'm having a bit of car trouble at the moment. Would you mind if we caught a taxi?'

'No problem. In the meantime, let's all go 'visit the cake'!' Mr. Parker extended his arm to his daughter and they both laughed.

THE WASH-HOUSE ROOSTER

Hilly says Mr. K. is a secret drinker, but we already know that. There's something in his pocket that clinks against the doorframe if he goes walking a bit crooked, or if he sits down too quickly in the kitchen chairs. Hilly says it's a bottle, just a little one. There's also that odd look he gets when he's remembering about the country he came from. That's Poland. I found it in the atlas and it's a long way from Australia. Late in the afternoons he sometimes starts talking in a way that's a bit harder to understand, about the war and other things. I suppose the secret about his drinking is really that he doesn't know we know about it.

Mum never mentions it. No one does. All of us don't say a thing — that's Mum and me, and also Iris Walker and Mrs. Prentiss who are our other boarders besides Mr. K. I tried to like Iris but she's such a busybody. She's so sly, dropping her little comments around like little seeds. As if we don't realise what she's doing. She leaves them sitting there a while like they're nothing important but she's always careful to come back to them again. Mum says I behave like a baby sometimes but what's Iris then? What's so bad about life that turns someone into that? Well, to her credit, even Iris hasn't said anything about Mr. K's drinking. Not out loud, that I know of.

I used to play hopscotch with Hilly. Her real name's Hilda but she hates it and I didn't want to tell her that I hate it too but it is kind of silly — silly Hilly — and no matter how much she tells her mother that she wants to be someone else, she's still called Hilda at home. Hilly and I gave up hopscotch. We reckon there's only so much you can do with jumping in and out and over boxes drawn in chalk and we're just about world champions anyway, so we're trying out hide-and-seek until we come up with a better game. My favourite spot to hide is in the big daisy bush by the wash-house. Hilly really hates flowers. She sneezes and coughs when she comes near them, so maybe it's a bit unfair of me, but she had a chance when we made the rules (no climbing on the roof or going out the front gate) so it's her fault. I make sure she's not around when she finally calls out that she's given up and then I crawl out from under the daisies and pretend I was somewhere else. I'll tell her one day, when I've got a better place that would be even harder to find.

Hilly says Iris is just lonely. She said she's trying to get attention. I don't know about Hilly; she's deep but she comes up with some weird things. I thought about it that night. I thought it might just be true but then Iris has got me and Mum and Mrs. Prentiss and Mr. K., so she can't be lonely. I explained it to Hilly but she was more interested in how long we could hold our breath so I never got a real answer. Holding our breath was before we settled on playing hide-and-seek.

Our rooster is a beauty. Horace. He looks like one of those big hats you see women wearing at fancy shows. The sort with lots of curved feathers hanging off them in all types of colours that shine and change in the light, except Horace is the kind of hat that walks around. He's got a strut when he walks and he thinks he owns the place. He likes to sit up on the roof of the washhouse in the backyard and look out over everything. If you come into the yard when he's in the garden, he runs around like you've invaded a special kingdom that he's supposed to guard. He crows and crows and stretches his neck up and shakes his feathers. He makes such a din. I love to watch him when he's doing his act. He doesn't do it for me though. I don't know why. Maybe I'm not scary enough. I have to wait for someone else to come into the backyard. He does it for just about everybody, except me … and Mr. K. and Mrs. Prentiss. They seem to have him bluffed somehow. The iceman can't stand him, though. The first time he came around the side of the house swinging a big chunk of ice in a hessian sling and calling out 'Ice-o!,' Horace went straight for him. The iceman left footprints right through the vegetable patch. He also left the ice there, a big wet block of it covered in dirt. Mum forgave Horace. She thinks he's glorious. That's the word she uses. Horace is my warning device when Hilly comes near me in the daisy bush. Hilly doesn't like him but she isn't frightened. She tells him to go away. Anyway, her little brother always told Hilly where I was hiding when we played the game in her garden so I reckon it's fair.

Iris doesn't like Mrs. Prentiss but then I think she doesn't like anyone much. She acts as if she likes Mum but I don't believe it. Mrs. Prentiss is all right but in a tough sort of way. She used to be a teacher. She's like my own schoolteacher I've got now but older, with her hair in a bun and very fussy about being neat and what's the right way to say things and all that. When Mum's not looking she moves the cutlery sometimes so it's in different places than where Mum put it, just moved around a bit. Mrs. Prentiss says she'll tell me how to remember cutlery but I don't care.

When Horace sees Mrs. Prentiss they stand there for a moment and then go in different directions. Horace doesn't say anything.

Mum told me once that Mrs. Prentiss had a husband but he died. She said not to ask Mrs. Prentiss about it. I wanted to know whether he was a pilot in the war or an explorer or famous for something but I didn't ask. Mrs. Prentiss has a photograph beside her bed but that man is a lot younger than her.

Mr. K. is from Poland, but I think I said that already. He came to Australia because they were being cruel in Poland. He didn't say what they did to be cruel but he says he's very happy here. When Horace sees Mr. K., he makes a quiet gurgly noise as if he's trying to remember the words to a rooster song and then seems to forget that Mr. K. is there.

I want to learn to spell Mr. K's name and he says he'll show me soon and then I'm going to look at it and learn how to say it properly. Iris sometimes looks at Mr. K. strangely, when he doesn't realise, as if she's thinking of something very special and she wants to know what it is. He's polite to everybody. Mum says he is a gentleman. His kind of work is very special and there aren't many jobs that can use his talents so he is waiting for the right one.

The postman doesn't bring anything for me but each month he brings a letter for Mr. K. with a strange stamp on it and I get the letter from the letterbox and take it to him. He says thank you very much in a polite way and takes it to his room. I don't know what the letters say but they make him sad for a while, so when another one came today I decided I would leave it in the letterbox and not tell him about it.

Iris was in the kitchen with Mum and I was doing my homework in the back room and I heard them talking. Iris said it wasn't right and something should be done. Iris said that it just wasn't good enough, especially for someone who was supposed to be a gentleman and what would other people think. Mum said she didn't want to be too hasty, but she said she would have a word and see what they said. Iris said I'm not saying they're up to no good and I'm not saying they aren't.

'It's when you go off to your Thursday bridge club,' she said. 'Mrs. Prentiss and Mr. K. go into the wash-house and they're in there alone for more than an hour,' she said.

I already knew they went in there. Everyone goes in there, when Horace will let them. I take the washing in there each morning. Mum goes in there to heat the copper and boil the water for the big clean twice a week. I don't know what the fuss is about. All of us poke around there sometimes for lost socks or to do a special wash. Iris was being strange but I could tell she had got Mum thinking.

Mum came back from her bridge game early. I saw her walking straight toward the wash-house but Horace kicked up a racket and she quickly turned around and came inside instead. She stood by the door and called Horace a name I didn't know. He flapped onto the clothesline and fluffed up his feathers so he looked twice as big as normal and then Mum laughed. She shook her head and I stuck mine back into my homework. My room is in the sleep-out at the back so later I saw Mr. K. come out of the wash house and after a few more minutes Mrs. Prentiss came out with a dress on a hanger but Mum didn't see.

That night we all sat down for our dinner. Iris got there after Mum and me and she gave Mum a funny look. Before Mum could say anything Mrs. Prentiss came in and Iris started playing with her napkin. Finally Mr. K. arrived and he was sitting up straight and smiling and he hadn't been drinking at all. We were just about to say grace when Mr. K. pulled an envelope from his pocket. It was the one I had left in the letterbox. He held it up in front of him and read out his name and address from it very slowly. Then he smiled and put the letter down and picked up the sauce bottle and read out the label. He got a few words wrong but his smile got bigger and bigger. Iris kept looking at Mum with that strange expression she had before, but with her brow more furrowed, and then back at Mr. K. All the time Mrs. Prentiss kind of perched there with a little grin of her own. Mr. K. picked up the cereal packet from the side cupboard and began to read the front of that to us.

Mum's eyes went wide for a moment. 'You mean ... you mean you couldn't read?!'

Mr. K's face was like a light. 'Dear lady,' he said, 'if it was not for my good friend, Mrs. Prentiss, giving me special lessons I would not be able to read this English to you today.'

He held the cereal packet to his chest while he was talking. Then he turned to Mrs. Prentiss and she blushed and looked down at the table.

'She has been so kind,' he said. 'Each week a special lesson how to read the English and I am getting all the time better I think. I have new words also. But I am so embarrassed not to read before so I ask her can she teach me in ... in ... private?'

Mum laughed. Iris coughed and accidentally knocked her knife from the table. Everyone was happy then and congratulating Mr. K. and Mrs. Prentiss, except Iris who suddenly began eating and I guess her mouth was too full to say much.

Mr. K. excused himself for a moment. He went to his room and came back with a bottle. It was tall and dark with a picture of a castle on the front. He placed it on the table like it was a trophy.

'Here, I give some wine for a special occasion.'

Mum straightened her back and pursed her lips for a moment before she replied. 'Thank you all the same, but we don't drink alcohol at the table.'

Iris narrowed her eyes and gave a kind of smile. Mr. K. moved the bottle to the sideboard.

'Well, it is for some other time then,' he said. 'We will celebrate my learning.'

*

The next Thursday, Hilly came over for the grand
championship hide-and-seek and while she was counting I snuck
over to my special place in the daisy bush. Horace was up on the
wash-house roof like a very important weather vane and he
looked down from the edge of the gutter while I squeezed under
the bush. I heard Hilly say coming ready or not but she headed
off in the wrong direction. Then I heard Mr. K. talking. He was
practising his English but I couldn't make out the words
properly. I crawled up to the wall and peeked in to the wash-
house through a little hole in the wood. I could see Mr. K's back
but I couldn't see Mrs. Prentiss properly. Smooth. I heard him
say smooth. Then he moved a bit to one side and I could see
Mrs. Prentiss. She had a happy face and her hair was all undone.
Mr. K.'s hand was running down her neck and she had her dress
very loose and her skin was all showing and his fingers went
onto the white of her chest and she closed her eyes. Yes, she
said, smooth, very good. I think Mr. K. is learning very quickly.

PLENTY

I'm a Big Girl. BG. It's my genes. I'm not slack and I don't over-eat. It's simply the way I am. Mum was big, and Dad too. On the other hand, some women are simply fat. You know — the don't-cares with their overflow muffin hips and flabby arms who blame it on their diet or the weather or their husbands or something. I'm Presentable with a capital P. That doesn't mean I don't cop some comments, because I'm average height but built large. I'm soft and elegant, though. I've got curves, and they go where they ought to go, just more so.

I could crush you. I'm probably twice whatever you are. I'm no bikini girl. I've got tits like basketballs, hips like barrels, thighs you can hardly wrap your arms round if you were burrowing your face between them, which I'm guessing you weren't thinking of until now. I take care of myself. Big and beautiful.

You won't find a tattoo anywhere on me; this me is enough. Only one scar, and I'm not telling you where. Call me vulgar; I don't care. I used to be embarrassed about my size, but not any more. It's *my* body, not anyone else's. Still, there are times now when I wonder why I should bother with attending to my appearance at all. But I do.

You've seen those primitive icons made of bone or stone, the ones they dig up from prehistoric times. Fertility goddesses. That's me, sort of, without the fertility. I don't know if I'd want kids if this were the only shape I could be. My doctor says there are too many risks. There, that's the downside. I do want the right guy plus a kid, but maybe life hasn't got that in store for me.

You might not think so but the pretty boys they want me. I'm a spell, peculiar. It's just that I don't want them. I know the man I want, and I knew him better once, much closer than we are now. We had our tender times, two of us at a restaurant or watching TV or sitting together and looking at the river. He didn't mind that my underwear was an industrial construction in lace. Actually, he mostly couldn't wait to get me undressed. We were all over the house back then, where there was space enough, anyway. Bed, couch, floor, garden, everywhere except the bath and shower really, where we couldn't both quite fit. He was smaller than me, what you'd call normal size, but he got breathless with me sitting on him. Me pumping away, and still being careful to hold him in, and my breasts bigger than his head all over his face but he starts to wane so we change positions and he's behind me and he's driving into me and we manage okay, better than okay. Much better. We always do.

But see, there I go, I'm back to present tense, and that's not healthy — those days are gone. I remember he especially liked to see me lying there, ready for oiling up and a night ... well, this is more than we need right now. You get the gist.

Let me explain love. Everyone has an idea of it, so why not me? It's crueller than you think. It gives you a taste, a sight of that life beyond this waiting and hoping, but it doesn't have to deliver. Sometimes a taste is all that you get. You wouldn't have the real blessing of it if it were guaranteed, if you could take it for granted now, would you? There'd be no need for love stories. Someone has to wait a while, strike a couple of obstacles on the path, and maybe a few of us have to miss out altogether so the others feel they have really won something. I have my charms, my beauty, but my chance feels like it's slipping away.

He had an appetite for me. He said I was abundant, a sign of plenty. I liked that. But it didn't last. She called him back just as easily as she had sent him packing, and he went. I had seen the photographs. That waif that she is, that stick figure, that nothing. Where was the siren in that call? It wasn't right.

I am still bones at heart. I was a skeleton once, itty-bitty. Was I there? I was there. I've seen the photos. A wee boney baby — thin, a little music box for my parents. And I did sing, still do. I sing the songs from my parents' country sometimes when we gather for a birthday feast or for Christmas, or a saint's day, though I don't know what most of them mean. I went to the old country for a wedding, and I had two proposals in one week. Fancy that. Both from big men, distant cousins. They promised me mad sex and lots of babies. I laughed. No future with them. Besides, they probably only wanted a life here, away from the hardship of their freezing northern winters and struggling economy. I shook my long hair, and I smiled and patted their big shoulders with my own wide hand. No, I said, you are sweet, but I am already promised to someone. A lie, maybe. I thought I might get him back, but that was dreaming, and where does dreaming get you?

It all changed though. I was flying home and trying to ignore the guy next to me who was making all those non-verbal complaints about having to fit next to someone my size. Passive aggressive. You know, the body language stuff — wriggle, jostle, elbow. I opened the in-flight magazine and the horoscope was right there, like fate. Who pays attention to them? I did, this time. For once it was speaking to me.

> *You are running but you need to stay. Turn and face your problem. If it is a matter of money, do not worry because it will soon come your way. If it is an affair of heart, the one who really loves you will be someone close, about to appreciate who you are and what you have to offer. You are coming into a time of plenty. Don't be shy.*

'Someone close' certainly wasn't the guy fidgeting around next to me. I knew who it was. And I didn't need the stars to tell me, though I'd probably needed that moment with a silly horoscope to make me wake up to myself right then. If his so-called wife couldn't face the truth before, then it was time she dealt with it. I went home just long enough to drop my bags and to shower and change. Then I drove straight here.

He's a creature of habit. Always leaves work at the same time. Any minute he will turn the corner of his street and pull into his driveway, where I am waiting. I don't want there to be any doubt. That's why I'm standing here naked, and ready. I am curvature and horizon and the beautiful bounty he needs. And my future is unlimited.

GOLDEN DAYS

As soon as she heard the tinkle of fine china behind her, Mitzi knew that Uncle William was back. Until then she had been inspecting his Royal Doultons and some quite tasteful Wedgwood in a large, glass-fronted cabinet, (locked, she noticed) and unaware that he had entered the room. From what Edward had told her, the good stuff had to be in another room, or in a vault somewhere. These pieces were very collectible but not quite top rank. Still, she would have to be careful. No point creating a bad impression. She turned and smiled.

William said nothing about her peering into the cabinet. He simply set the tray on the table and beckoned his visitors towards their chairs. Edward settled into his chair, as Mitzi maintained a feline smile and slid gracefully onto the seat next to him. The plume of steam from the teapot leant its own sinuous aspect. William nudged the tray to the centre of the table and creakily sank into his own, battered leather tub.

'So good to see you, Uncle William,' said Edward.

'What have you been doing lately, Mitzi?' William said. 'You don't get to Melbourne often. Are you seeing the sights?'

Mitzi registered the slight. She paused, the teacup at her lips, and replayed Uncle William's words in her mind for a moment.

He had not acknowledged Edward's comment, she thought, but perhaps that was being too cautious.

'Well, I've done a little shopping, of course. I was going to visit the gallery but you know how it is: never enough time.'

'Ah, the gallery is a good idea. Do you know 'The Banquet of Cleopatra' by Tiepolo. One of my favourites, though I really do like the Streetons.'

Edward realised with surprise that he knew the Tiepolo painting. Someone had sent him a postcard of it earlier that year. He immediately piped up.

'Yes, I love it too! Cleopatra!'

He turned to Mitzi to show he was sharing a special knowledge with William, an intimate moment that might be to their advantage.

'It's quite large. Cleopatra has put on a feast to impress someone; Marc Antony, I think. He's at one end of the table with his retinue and she's sitting at the other just about to drop a pearl into her glass of wine.'

Mitzi frowned.

'A pearl? Why would anyone do a silly thing like that?'

'To dissolve it. You know, to show how little a pearl means to her. Wonderful painting.'

Edward turned back towards Uncle William and was pleased with the small smile he saw.

'Wonderful painting,' Edward repeated, and picked up the nearest pastry concoction with a delicate pincer movement of thumb and forefinger. He looked at his uncle again. 'You made these?'

As far as Edward knew, Uncle William had never had to cook in his life but there had been no sign of the usual house-help since he and Mitzi had arrived. In fact the whole place had a run-down air. It was faintly possible that his uncle had cooked them after all. William did seem quite proud of his offering, and it was best to be safe.

'They look lovely,' Mitzi added.

Still, as Edward looked at the glistening little cake in his hand and the rows of others before him, he thought there was something odd about them. His uncle quickly took one for himself and motioned his guests towards the tray.

'As many as you like. The little ones on your side are especially nice.'

'Mmm, they do look good.'

Mitzi's long fingers hovered over the tray. Finally, she scooped up what she gauged to be the smallest cake and took a delicate bite.

Edward knew his uncle had been a sharp operator in his time but after Aunt Megan had died, William had gradually lost interest in business. The family company had been sold. William had cashed up and retired. Edward vaguely remembered his aunt. She had taken a shine to him during his occasional childhood visits, he thought. Perhaps it was because they had no children of their own.

Uncle William's shaking hand reached for another cake. The old man was quite ill now and there would never be a better time to visit. They could talk to him before he got too scatty, before anyone else came onto the scene and gave him the wrong advice.

William seemed to like these cakes quite a lot. Edward also took another one.

'Lovely, Uncle. Quite delicious! The texture is ... unusual. This shiny part, what is it?'

'Yes,' Mitzi, chimed in. 'I don't think I've ever had any quite like this before.'

She slowly pushed a stray crumb into her mouth, holding William's gaze as she did so, ever so gradually dialling up the charm. Despite herself, she reached for one more.

'Another?'

The tray quivered in Uncle William's hands as Edward took one. He hoped there would be a longer moment of communion with his uncle, a chance to earn his trust. Not about art, though. He didn't want to expose his ignorance there. It was time to steer the topic to money, though gently, of course. He contented himself with his uncle's smile for the moment, then launched into the real reason for his visit.

'Uncle, the last time I rang, you mentioned investments and said that ...'

'Actually, Edward, I think you raised the subject.'

Edward realised that Uncle William rocked slightly most of the time, rather like sheep do when they stand in one spot. William's lower lip also shook a little, even when he was eating. A large crumb danced there at that moment, exaggerating the movement. Poor old bugger. Well, rich old bugger, actually. Edward fought back a grin at his unspoken joke.

'Really, Uncle? Oh, I forget. Never mind. Anyway, Mitzi and I have been doing quite well in real estate for some time now, haven't we, dear? One must be careful but we have been

— there are so many sharks. The Ivory Court development was good for us, wasn't it, Mitz?'

Edward hoped that using the diminutive of his wife's name would signal a more intimate exchange, but his uncle gave no new sign of warming to them yet. Nonetheless, Edward had broached the matter of money, and he couldn't draw back now.

'When I rang, Uncle, you mentioned that you'd always put your money into gold and, well, you've seen what's happened to that market recently. Even the government's selling. I wanted to help you, to offer some advice.'

William nodded. Edward sensed that he was on the right track now and decided to get straight to the point.

'There's just no reason to stay in gold any more, Uncle. Mitzi and I haven't seen as much of you as we would have liked in the last few years, us being in Sydney and all, and we, well, we thought the best way to make amends was to give you this chance to come in with us on our new project. We know you're not well and it would be our way of looking after you, making sure you were okay financially.'

It was Mitzi's turn. She put down her cup and locked Uncle William in her sweetest gaze.

'Yes, it would be perfect, Uncle. With what we know about the property market and that extra bit of capital from you, there's so much we could be doing together. You'd never have to worry about money again. We'd be able to see each other much more often too.' She rolled a curl of her long hair around one finger and held the tip to the corner of her mouth. 'We'd move down from Sydney and buy a place here for ourselves. We could be close by. In fact, we could even stay here with you, if you liked — take care of you. Aunt Megan would have liked that.'

Uncle William moved back in his chair. Edward and Mitzi beamed powerfully at him, focusing promises of good fortune and companionship at him. Finally, the old man leant forward and cleared his throat. Edward wiped his hands surreptitiously on his trousers.

'So kind of you to look me up after all this time, Edward. More cake?'

Edward didn't understand. Was this a No? He licked his lips.

'Our pleasure, Uncle.'

He took another of the gleaming pastries.

'And about the project, I have the figures. I can show you right here. You'd never regret it.'

'Oh, I know I won't.'

Edward struggled. That wasn't really an acceptance but it wasn't a clear rejection either. William had always been an astute investor. Edward began to worry.

'What is it, Uncle? You got out of gold already? You sold up?'

Edward's nose wrinkled slightly, involuntarily, lifting his glasses for a second. There would still be money, Edward thought. Somewhere. There had to be, whatever it was invested in now, he was sure he could talk the old bastard around.

'No, in fact I put everything that I had left *into* gold. Everything. Not the house and some of the contents, of course. Got to have somewhere to live ... and die!'

William laughed at his little jest — a short, coarse rasp that echoed somewhere in his scrawny chest.

'The house and the collectibles, the ones I haven't sold, are only mine in trust now. The Doultons and the Josiahs, the Dobells and the Nolans and all that. I've left them to the Salvation Army and the State Art Gallery. You don't know what a job it was to get all that sorted out.'

Edward was disappointed about the house and the collections but oddly relieved also. This simplified things, and he was chasing bigger fish, after all. The old man's gold would still be worth a fortune.

'Everything into gold, you say?'

'Yes. There wasn't as much as I expected, what with medical bills and all, but yes.' Uncle William leant forward with some difficulty. 'Do you know the Japanese custom, Edward?'

Mitzi was dumbstruck. She hoped Edward would be able to work out what was happening and quickly; the old man was rambling. Edward squinted but said nothing.

'Gold is a beautiful thing, Edward. From the look of your watch and Mitzi's bracelet, I'd say you know that. It has some extraordinary properties too. Did you know that just an ounce of gold can be spread so finely it could make a thread eighty kilometres long? It's so malleable.'

"Like gold to ayery thinnesse beate."

Mitzi was amazed to hear her own voice. She hadn't remembered that line since her school days.

'Well chosen, Mitzi. John Donne; talking about the parting of lovers, I think. Your Aunt Meg loved that poem.'

William paused for another coughing episode, patting a handkerchief to his mouth. He exhaled, weariness etched in the lines around his eyes. 'Anyway, the Japanese, through boredom or extravagance or maybe a bit of both, sometimes dress up their food with gold foil. It's inert; harmless in your gut, and it looks so pretty. Great way to show off to your friends too. It's taken me nearly two years to get through it all. That's how long the doctors said I had left. You can put it on so many different foods but I really like it best on these.'

William lifted the last cake and turned it to glisten in the light. He winked at Mitzi, then opened his mouth, and swallowed everything.

14 PALMER ROAD

The fat man sat with my father in our front room, refusing cups of tea and the scones my mother had quickly made. It was just before Christmas in 1968, the middle of a record heat wave, and far too hot for the dark blue suit he wore. Mum fussed in the kitchen and let me devour all the scones with their glistening knobs of apricot jam. When the visitor left, my parents left the house, retreating to the garden where they pretended to check the tomatoes. I knew this ritual. Over tea that night Dad announced that he had been made regional manager at the State Head Office. We were moving again.

This time, at least, we were going back to the city. Because they wanted me to start the new school year there, my parents rang Aunt May and arranged that I board with her at Palmer Road. It would only be for a few months, they said, until they sold our current house.

For ten years we had moved about the country. Each December I'd start paying more attention to my parents' conversations, listening for clues. Listening in the hope that we might stay in the same town two years in a row, but we rarely did. Dad would be transferred to another country town, further out in the wheat belt perhaps. They were always sending him in to trouble-shoot, to replace their failed or retiring staff, to lift sales or establish new territory. There would be a new job title and sometimes a pay rise. Each success, though, meant his work was finished. Each December, the removal trucks sat just around the corner, already waiting. Fishing town, mining town, farming centre — new school, new school, new school. I got good at packing and good at leaving things behind. I could live with less than most people I knew. The city would be fine.

Mum cried as we waited at the bus stop in the middle of town. Dad was already out on the road somewhere, heading for his first appointment. Mum kept asking me to repeat her instructions for catching the train once I had arrived in Adelaide. I felt like a six-year-old being drilled before an errand. I was surprised she didn't tie the train fare into the corner of my handkerchief. She continually checked her watch and looked down the road for the bus. When it did arrive, I kissed her quickly and took a window seat. I sat there, high above her, giving her a smile which I hoped combined the right air of affectionate concern and maturity until the air brakes hissed and we pulled away. She grew smaller behind me, waving to the last.

A sweating old man from Coober Pedy sat next to me. He continually wrestled with his newspaper, rustling and refolding it with extravagant arm movements. Every few minutes he made a weird snorting noise. Five hours to go. I leant against the window frame and looked outside. My companion talked to his paper, muttering over a crossword puzzle as the dry paddocks rolled past. In the luggage hold below us was the suitcase my parents had given me. My own suitcase. A rite of passage? It was cheap — even I could tell that — but it had been well cared for. There was a slight scuff on one corner, which I'd kept my hand over when giving it to the driver for storage. Afterwards I felt embarrassed to have been so embarrassed; so proud. Inside the lid was an old and peeling sticker from the Grosvenor Hotel in Adelaide. My parents' honeymoon. I thought of them side by side in one of those little rooms so long ago, newly married, the same suitcase full of their clothes. There was a trick to the left-hand catch. You had to get it just so. Not that there was any great discovery waiting when it did open. It held two school uniforms, a weekend's worth of casual clothes, my blue plastic crystal radio set and a copy of *Gulliver's Travels*. I watched the paint lines on the road and let the dull sound of the bus engine lull me. The telegraph poles flicked by. The lazy arcs of the wires dipped and rose in hypnotic rhythm.

The little girl steps out of the back door of the house. There is the noise of a party inside, the squeals and laughs of other small children until the door closes behind her. A single light arches its neck over the porch. I see the flounces of her dress. A mass of petticoats corrugates around her stockinged legs like a white carnation, but she is not dressed for this winter, not for the outdoors. I see her breath hanging in the air, and her sudden shiver. She steps off the porch and walks down the path towards the back of the yard where it is darker. Perhaps she is going to hide. Perhaps she has a surprise gift to retrieve. Near the end of the yard the lawn drops away into shadow where there is the sound of running water. She leaves the path and walks across the icy shine of the grass but she is having more trouble keeping her footing. It happens quickly. Her polished shoes slide sideways for an instant and her arms jerk up instinctively for balance, as if to grab for an overhead branch, but there isn't one. She topples off the bank and is under the water in an instant. Her hair trails and her white party dress moves in a swirl, slow as clouds. She thinks she will go back to the party soon. She thinks she will step out and walk back up the lawn. But it is cool and drowsy down there. The light on the back porch grows dimmer.

The bus hissed and jerked. I lurched forward, out of my dream. The same paddocks as before were spread outside, it seemed — the same roadside fringe of scrubby trees. The man next to me issued the same grunts and snorts. I looked at his watch as he snapped the newspaper and realised I was only half an hour closer to Adelaide.

Where was she going, anyway? Was she still down there, waiting her time to rise from the creek or stream or whatever it was? I wanted a drink.

I tried to remember Palmer Road. Aunt May bought the 1920s bungalow in a dead-end street; busy main road at one end, train line at the other. She wanted to rent it out for a while so my parents had jammed their blue Singer saloon with all their possessions, including me, and shifted from their small beachside flat into number 14. I had just turned two.

I knew the kitchen best; the cool linoleum under my chubby hands and knees and feet, the humming white cliff face of the Kelvinator fridge looming above me, the heat of the wide enamel-fronted stove, the daily setting and clearing of the laminex table while I clung to one of its chrome legs. The kitchen was the real home. It was where Mum was. It was where

Dad sat as soon as he arrived from work and where we were when he broke the news. I barely understood what was happening then but I would become used to it. This news of moving.

A huge truck squeezed into the driveway at number 14 back then, scraping paint off the gatepost and flattening a rosebush as it reversed towards the front door. The tail swung open, revealing a huge empty space. I stood at the lip of a ramp staring into that space until a man in blue overalls shooed me away. The house spilt itself onto the floor. Clothes, dishes, shoes. My toys were stacked into boxes, unreachable. Mum hoisted me onto her lap and shut the car door. Dad slipped the Singer into gear and we drove away.

Palmer Road was lined with jacaranda trees, their blossoms littering the footpath and crunching under my shoes. Number 14. A Californian bungalow with glazed bull-nose capping on the wide veranda wall. The house was smaller than I expected. Roses bordered a ragged half moon of lawn in the front yard. Pigeons murmured in the pair of tall pencil pines that stood on either side of the driveway. I dropped my case by the front door and knocked.

Unlike the house, Aunt May was bigger than I recalled. She filled the doorway, wiping her hands on an apron.

'Ah, you got here then. Come inside. You must be tired.'

She turned back into the hallway and I picked up my case, following as far as the third door.

'You pop in there now and I'll call you for tea in a while.'

It was a small bedroom with an old single bed by the window. Next to the bed was a dresser. The only item on it was a traveller's alarm clock, the kind you fold into a small case. There was a narrow dark wardrobe and, on the wall, a framed embroidery; 'The Lord is my Shepherd'. I pulled the curtains back. The window looked out to a wooden fence and the neighbour's red brick wall. I put my suitcase on the bed's chenille spread, fiddled the left catch and emptied it. The radio and book looked meagre on the dresser, like the ornaments of a rather ascetic religion on an altar.

That night I lay in bed and listened to the sound of trains. The city was busy but I liked the continual background hum of its activity. In the country there had been such stillness you could hear a car approaching town for miles.

In the morning Aunt May showed me the hand-propelled mower.

'Since you're here, I'll just get you to mow the lawn. I'm off to the shop a while. Do a good job now!'

Aunt May knew how to wield a word. She had 'just' down to perfection. Just clean the gutters. Just post the mail. Just wash the floor. Just do it. 'Just' made anything possible.

We got on all right though. She had her rituals and I learnt to fit in. In the morning there would be half an hour of music from a large round Bakelite radio on top of the refrigerator. The radio was big and as curvaceous as a 1950s Buick or Hollywood starlet. I played the two images back and forth, unable to choose between them. Eventually I put the starlet in the Buick. Thirty minutes was the unstated limit for the radio. I speculated whether this was part of her religious belief, or based on some wacky new theory about the evil effects of radio waves. When I tried turning it on after school she calmly flicked it off again.

'You don't want to be listening to that now.'

Her meals were plain and spongy. She boiled all her food into submission. Meat, potatoes, carrots steamed to a grey similarity. A treat would be a shared tin of peaches afterwards. I stole spoonfuls of condensed milk from the refrigerator when she wasn't around.

Aunt May was not a conversationalist. In the evening she liked to watch two quiz shows and then turned the TV off for an hour's reading. She went to bed early. It was so quiet at night. I hooked the aerial of the crystal radio up to the curtain rod in my room but had trouble dialling anything in for long. A snatch of music and then it would slide off into static. Mostly I read or did my homework. Alarm clock, shower, train to school, train from school, meal, homework, bed.

My hormones were doing wicked things. I fell in love with a different girl on the train each day. I had to relieve the tension. I decided to steal a girlie magazine from the local corner shop one evening when Aunt May sent me there for butter. The girl on the cover combined a pouting come here-go away look with an enormous cleavage. This would be the one. I slipped it under my school jumper, my heart racing. Instead of the middle-aged Greek owner it was his sixteen-year-old daughter waiting at the counter. I didn't have the nerve. While she got the butter I snuck the magazine back onto the rack and ran out on to the footpath. All that and I hadn't even got past the cover. At the front gate of number 14, I realised I had left the butter behind and would have to return to the shop. The daughter was still there, smiling, sweet, and very plain.

Aunt May's house was *Chez Nous*. It said so on a brass plaque fixed by the front door. Next door was *Emoh Ruo*, and other houses had names that were also lame riddles, but often indecipherable. The most intriguing houses to me were those without a name. How many *Chez Nous* in Clarence Park, I wondered? I considered a survey of them as a school project.

Boredom. I used my hours to explore the house. Over the course of a few weeks I found where everything was, not that this advantaged me. There was nothing exciting to be found. Her pills, her vast underwear, the coupons and lottery tickets, the sherry bottle behind the encyclopedia. I was tempted to try the sherry but I was sure she would have a mark somewhere on the bottle. I knew where Aunt May kept her money too. If I had wanted it, really wanted it, I could have opened the old biscuit tin and taken her rainy day cash. Could have, but she was always watching. Not by standing guard over it personally or keeping an eye on me. She had a better way. She used all the force of her trust. Money promised the sophistication and ritual of opening cigarette packets, tearing the cellophane, unfolding the foil cover and drawing the first perfect cylinder out. But I couldn't touch her money. The sophistication of a smoking life would have to wait.

After school I sat on the veranda and waited for the girl on the corner to pass by. I had seen her before. Small and blonde, she tilted her head down a little as she walked her spaniel past the house each night but there was a shy smile also. It took two weeks for me to speak to her. I contrived to be near the gate and said something flattering about the dog. We started talking immediately. Later she told me she'd just about given up walking the thing each night because I had taken so long to speak to her.

From then on I had trouble concentrating at school. I would scoff my food when I got home and dash through my homework, tell Aunt May I was going for a walk and head straight for the jacaranda at the dead end of the street. Pam would be waiting. We walked the neighbourhood each night for a couple of hours, hand in hand, talking. We kissed as the lights of the nine o'clock train flashed over us and then we parted. A real girl to talk with and smell and hold, to dream about as I lay back in my bed.

Aunt May was going to the pictures. She gave me her customary reminders about locking up, washing the dishes, and not watching the TV too long as I saw her to the front door. I tried not to seem too eager as I helped her arms into the sleeves of her coat. She pecked me on the cheek and set off. Halfway down the driveway she turned back and I thought she had changed her mind. Instead, she collected a hat. It was pink and round, a cascade of tiny flowers on one side. It reminded me of a cake.

'Forget my head if it wasn't screwed on!'

Another peck and then she paused to look at my face. Did she know? Could she tell? She furrowed her brow, pulled a hankie from her sleeve and licked a corner. I recognised the motion and as she reached to clean a newly imagined spot on my cheek, I took a step back.

'Have a good time, Aunt May.' I tried to sound firm.

She pressed her lips together. 'Hmmm. Remember to lock up now.'

I rang Pam. She came over in an instant and we sat on the lounge, awkwardly close.

'I've got my new underwear on. It's great. Mum'll kill me when she sees I snagged the knickers, though. Did it climbing through a fence last night. Want to see?'

She lifted the edge of her white dress too briefly. There was a flash of pale blue material with a lace trim.

'I'm bored,' she said. 'I want to do something new. I want to do something different.'

Where could we go around here, I wondered? There was nothing, unless … One morning at the breakfast table I'd felt a round bump under my foot, something hard beneath the linoleum. I'd waited until Aunt May was out and moved the table to get at it. It was the ring-handle for a cellar door, something she had never mentioned.

'I know a place,' I said. 'It's a secret. What will you do if I show you?'

Pam looked away and played with the bottom of her skirt for a moment.

'That depends. Have you touched a girl before?' She looked up. 'I mean, really touched a girl?'

I forced my mouth to shut.

*

That evening Aunt May slid a bowl of dessert in front of me and went back to the sink.

'Are you feeling all right?' she said over her shoulder. 'You should eat up, you know. Growing boy. You need your strength.'

The kitchen floated on a box of air. The floor felt so flimsy, I was sitting on the skin of a drum. My mouth was dry. I jammed a spoonful of the custard into it. A dark space swam beneath me.

FISHING

I dump the stack of files onto my office desk and slump into the chair. I'm three hours into a Saturday morning when I should have been having breakfast with Sally and the kids; when I should have been walking to the park with the dog, buying a coffee at the corner shop, bringing the newspaper home.

That's Sally and the children in the photo on my noticeboard, at the beach where we used to go out on Dad's boat. Just enough room for the five of us in it, Dad proudly at the helm, as always. You can see Dad is squinting under the peak of his hat in this other shot. Really hot when that one was taken. He's holding up a big pair of King George Whiting we had for dinner that same day. I miss those times, and him. He loved that little boat.

Anyway — no breakfast, no walk, no newspaper or corner-shop coffee. Now it's just page upon page of the Witherspoon spreadsheet in all its glory. The dividend summary for the third quarter completely fills the computer screen and there are more than twenty other files to check through today.

A slight flicker in the screen catches my eye; small enough to make me squint and watch more closely — in case I was mistaken. In case it had simply been a reflection of the fluorescent light overhead above. But it's definitely there. It would be more annoying if it was really pronounced but I can live with it for now — get this job over with and leave a message to call the technician on Monday.

Besides, a little glitch like that reminds me that technology is not perfect. Perhaps more pleasingly, it has distracted me a while longer from tackling the stack of folders. Just pray the machine doesn't crash. I save the file again, to be sure.

The Witherspoon account. What kind of fool would promise to prepare a complete analysis of the investment portfolio in just two days? This kind. And then the first day was chewed up when the Jurgensen financial statements turned out to be a nightmare. Forgive me, Sally.

There it is again. Somewhere in that display of several hundred cells the movement begins, an almost instantaneous shiver of the whole matrix. Like a nervous twitch. I never quite catch where it begins; that's somewhere off to the side of my vision each time. A little wave tickles my sight before I've fully registered that it's happening, and it quickly washes over the screen.

How do I start this job? I've done hundreds like it before. Should be easy. I open the crisp manila folder of the first month's reports. Row upon row of numbers. My eyes pull back to the screen and those faint but regular lines in the panel of light. The flicker once more. It reminds me of my father's advice. If the surface of the water changes momentarily, you could do worse than move your line to that spot. A fish moving just below it perhaps. I slowly wind in the line and flick it back out in a lazy arc to land just where the shimmering had caught my eye. Dad coughs, quietly, as if afraid he'll scare them off but no fish are biting yet. This is a day for sitting and watching the calm gloss around our small boat, for the shared silence of a rare time together. The fish don't really matter. I settle back in the boat and listen to the soft lap of the water against its side, the fishing rod loose in my hands. All the time in the world.

THE CITY-BAY TRAM

The City-Bay tram wants to be Trinidadian, sweet metal music like a steel band, but the sound of it passing is a wall of tin cans falling, a thousand scissors sharpening, an argument that ends with a cutlery set being thrown down a flight of stairs. I lie in my bed at night, two houses from the track, and listen to its clattering song repeat every few minutes until midnight. By sunrise, the Doppler refrain has started again, often with the up-track and down-track trams syncopating their clanking rhythms as they meet. The familiar calamitous noise, that ungraceful percussion, better than any softer tune.

In the morning I snatch breakfast, then close the front gate and walk towards the nearest stop. The sun is still weak in an overcast sky. The headlights of the next tram to the city are just bright dots down the track when I leave the house, so far away they seem not to be moving. I pull my coat tight and walk briskly, listening for the sound of the approaching tram behind me. A few minutes later the bells of the nearby crossing clang like persistent dinner gongs. I speed up my walking and reach the stop just as the tram arrives. Its accordion doors fold back and I step up into the lacquered wood-trim of a panelled board-room, embellished with the chrome flashes and vinyl seats of a 1960 Holden Special. There isn't much room but I find a place beside a large woman in a purple cardigan. She is flicking through a magazine and ignores me.

Where are you now?

Autumn morning is schoolbags, handbags, newspapers and still-damp hair. The day's first rush is over but there are dozens of school kids on an excursion. We're all squeezed in, no room for knees. The backs of seats will be fronts flipped for the return trip. The kids discover this and want the seats in constant motion despite the crush. The tram jerks forward, shaking like a sleep-out in a storm. The kids chatter. They twist in their seats and jostle each other. The adults sit still, shoulder to shoulder, crowded and alone. They seldom talk to each other. The man nearest the rear door has a small patch of dried shaving cream on his left earlobe. When the pretty girl opposite him looks elsewhere he drinks her in. Despite the children's noise, I hear the woman across the aisle minutely dissect the scandalous life of a talk-show host. A man like that! His wife is pregnant and he's having a fling with that woman from *Blue Dream*, the tall one, you know. And not just one mistress, but two! There was that designer he was seeing back in Perth. How can he carry on like nothing has happened? Her companion nods and responds but her answers are half of a different conversation. Her son is leaving home. Her husband doesn't listen to her any more. She laments the weather in her bones. The rest of us eavesdrop, bury ourselves in books or gaze at the world passing outside the window.

If you were here, we would have exchanged a whisper, dug elbows into each other's side.

The private is made public in backyards by the tramline. Limp washing and weedy kingdoms, corrugated iron roofs with a rash of red rust, lean-to laundries and riotous gardens, decrepit sheds and slow-moving men in cardigans who will not be leaving for work. Excited dogs leap at fences as we pass. When the tram climbs the bridge over the railway track, I look down into Ingham's Plaster Works. The concrete floor of the yard is dusted with white icing sugar. Two men in overalls stand there like odd figurines on a wedding cake. They are pale with plaster powder to their waists where their true colours begin to appear, as if they have been partly dipped in flour. Then they stoop, lift a long flexing piece of plaster and carry it to a drying rack under a shelter. Large ceiling roses are already stacked there like ornate plates.

The tram's a corridor ten kilometres long which the conductor walks every day.

Any fares? Any fares?

His leather bag a paunch for change and tickets. I buy my ticket and look back out the window. I've marked every day of your absence on the itinerary you stuck to my refrigerator. I've known exactly where you were every day for two months — each city, each gallery and museum you visited, even without postcards. Writing just isn't me but I'll always be thinking of you, you had said. I squint over the horizon and see you in Rome, hailing a taxi to the airport. Your hair swings in a ponytail, your one bag is slung on your back. How do you manage to travel so light? Then you're sinking into the seat as the long jet peels away from Italy and Europe and over a dark bank of clouds. You don't look out. Then I see you putting down a magazine and closing your eyes. By now your plane is only hours from home.

I wanted to meet you at the airport. I hate airports as much as you hate writing letters but I was going to be there. You warned me off. Too many delayed flights, you said. You'll get all wound up waiting and you'll be in a mood, you said. I'll just get in when I get in and catch a taxi, you said. It'll be better that way.

I check the address of the bookshop. It's windows I want. Books about windows. Especially those about paintings of windows. Before you left you hung your newest work, a vast painting of a window in my lounge room. Hung it over a real window that faces my street. Now I have a permanently mid-afternoon view of a harbour with water like wet paint instead of the real fence, the real trees, the real cable that guides the City-to-Bay tram past our house. Small white boats against all that blue. I think it's a picture of a harbour in Spain but I don't know why. You were a long time in Spain during your last trip; almost didn't want to come back.

When I rang and told him what I was after, the owner of the shop was sure he had something special you would like. It was expensive but I said yes straight away. He put it aside. I'm going to leave it on the bed, so it will be waiting for you when your taxi arrives. I'll find a picture in it that I hope you'll like and I'll open the book and leave it there like a window into some other world, a hole in the bed we can both fall through.

Just before I left the house I rang the airline and checked your flight would be on time. I imagine you walking into the terminal this evening and suddenly I want to see you so much more. I think of going to meet you there after all but I know I won't. Not when you've said no.

The conductor returns, swaying with the movement of the tram as he calls for fares. Below me the spoked pulley-wheels of this treadle sewing machine drag the ground away. On the roof are metal antlers; antennae that siphon blue electric juice from a long slack-wire no one ever walks.

The woman alongside me pulls an orange from her bag and slices it into quarters with a small wooden-handled knife. She's done this before. The quarters are cut into eighths. She lifts a little arc of bright flesh to her mouth and it disappears, everything. The skin of the orange is in there — thick, glossy, unchewable. But she chews it. Then the next piece. Eating everything. I think of you, and honey.

The tram approaches the terminus in Victoria Square, the middle of the city. Kids scrabble for their bags and jam the aisle. I wait for their mad exit to finish. The cold bites into my skin as I step down to the ground. Winter soon. In the middle of the city square is Queen Victoria's statue. She is sensibly layered in a heavy bell of dresses and petticoats. She scowls at the modern fountain across the road where sculpted figures of men and women stretch themselves naked and wet under arcs of water. The wind lifts spray into the air and across the worn paving. My shoes slip on the surface as I walk towards the shop.

I find it in a narrow street near the Central Market. The large glass windows are tinted to protect the books from sunlight. How would you like these windows? I remember a painting in

Los Angeles that took up the whole of the side of a building opposite a vacant lot that was used as a car park. The painting made the bare brick wall into something else. It became a modern glassy office building that reflected its surroundings. In the painted reflection was a view of the future, where the parking lot was empty but for the burnt shell of a car and two sheep picking at weeds that had burst through ruined asphalt.

No one is behind the counter or anywhere nearby. I ring the bell and an elderly man appears from a door at the back. He must be over seventy, tall, upright, dressed for something much more formal than selling books. His jacket is houndstooth, his shoes gleam impossibly, his tie speaks of a club I'll never know. He is friendly but he is not the man I spoke with on the telephone. When I ask for the book of window paintings there is a flicker of hesitation before he turns to a shelf behind the counter. He rummages among books wrapped in brown paper, books with slips of paper saying 'Heathcote Tuesday' or 'Jensen Friday p.m.' He rifles through them twice. He is sorry but his son is normally there and had to go out and he doesn't know what could have happened to it. Paintings of windows? A large book? His son will be back tomorrow. He casts a sorrowful look over his shoulder at the shelf of books put by for promises. We both know it isn't there. I can't tell him tomorrow will be too late. That would not make the book appear.

I pretend to browse, hoping the book is still in the Art section. Perhaps it has been put away by mistake. It's not there. I leave the warmth and step into the street.

The next few shops I try don't have it either. Sales assistants consult their lists and ring each other but I can't give them enough details to convince them the book exists. There are a couple of maybes and some we-could-order-this-one-and-see-if-it's-what-you-wanteds. The morning passes in walking back and forth across the shopping district, following fruitless suggestions. The owner of First Editions, a small place reached by two flights of rickety stairs, listens politely but after a minute something in his eyes shows he has lost interest, that it is just too hard. The bookshop at the Art Gallery has nothing even close to what I want. I buy a coffee and cake at Café Buongiorno and sit in its shelter for a while, working out where else I can look.

The assistant at Back Pages raises her one eyebrow as if to say I have just won Stupid Question of the Day. Her green fingernails slowly drum the counter and I retreat, glancing across the shelves as I leave, in the vague hope that it will be there, waiting to catch my attention. The shelves at Artworks are full of books of paintings. I tell myself it will be here. The manager crooks an index finger across his lips and thinks.

'Windows. You don't mean Hopper?'

I wonder if he is making a bad joke to test me.

'No,' I say, 'not Hopper. And not Magritte. It isn't just one artist. It's a whole book on paintings of windows by all sorts of artists.'

He shakes his head.

The sun is striking biscuity tones on the stonework of the old government buildings in King William Street and I still have three more shops to go. There is a glimmer of recognition at one but it turns out to be another book on church stained-glass.

After two more hours of traipsing through bookstores, I'm back in Victoria Square.

*

The tram home is a box of windows that fractures light across shuddering fences. That irony is not lost on me. There's no morning horde of clamouring kids. Just half a dozen strangers being chauffeured home in a long lurching pram that's going lickety-split. There and back, there and back — its rough rhythm loose as the rhyme of a half-remembered song. I'll be home with less than an hour to spare before you're due and I have nothing to give you.

I used to ride the tram on summer afternoons as a kid. Fishing rod and bucket balanced against my shoulder for the ride to Glenelg, a breeze through the window tossing my hair about. The tram seemed old and frail even then, a beachside shack that had grown wheels, a big billy-cart trundling to the sea, coming to salt air, to tribes of ice-cream wielders, to fish and chips in newspaper wrapping, to scalding sun, and a lurching halt at the jetty.

When I step off, there is a hint of rain. The tram hisses into the distance, a blue cascade of thorny sparks running the wires the rest of the way down to the sea.

There is a letter sticking out of the box, one end damp from an afternoon shower. It's so long since I have seen your writing, it takes me a moment to recognise it.

The house is dark. I pull the curtains across the windows, turn on a light and set the letter on the dinner table. I stare at it a while, wanting to open it, resisting. Instead, I make the bed, then cook dinner and leave it warm in the oven. I move the letter to one side while I set the table for our first meal together again. I try the television news but it is all trivial politics and football, so I turn it off. The rumble of trams plays in the background as I clean up the house.

I lift up the letter again and smell it, but there's no trace of your perfume on it. The stamp is familiar. I switch the oven off and go to sit by your painting. White boats and blue water. Like the stamp. There's been no tram for an hour. The last flight into town arrived two hours ago.

MINOR KEY

'Stop the car!'

I was thinking about what she had said a minute earlier, and not listening properly but it only took a millisecond to jump out of that. She was loud, insistent, shrieking.

'Stop the car! Stop the car!'

I hauled at the steering wheel, and the car slewed sideways on the dirt road. I felt it pitching hard though and imagined it already rolling, our imminent deaths in this remote place — glass, torn metal, blood, and her words slicing through the white noise of coming oblivion. But the complaining tyres and the dust and scramble of my hands at the wheel kept us upright, somehow. We slid into the softer ground at the edge of the road and, instead of flipping, the car shuddered to a noisy halt. Luck and instinct. There was the sound of stones falling back to earth, and silence.

She had her face in her hands, crying or laughing.

'Jesus,' she said into her fingers. 'Jesus, fucking Jesus. What is that? Is that what I think it is?'

I looked from her to the world outside.

'It is.'

She stared through my side window at the hulking piano that sat next to the car.

'Yeah.'

'You alright?' I asked.

She opened her door. 'Let's go and see. It's fallen off a trailer I reckon.'

'Of course. And landed upright, without a scratch.'

'It's in the middle of the damned road, for God's sake.'

She walked around it slowly, running one finger through the light film of dust. 'Hasn't been here long.'

'Thank you, Detective Georgie,' I joked, but she didn't smile.

'Go on, play something.'

'I can't.'

'You told me you could. You had lessons.'

'I was ten years old,' I said. 'Give me a break.'

But she didn't, just tilted her head a little and gave me that steady gaze instead. So I lifted the lid and stroked the keys. Weirdly, it was pretty well in tune. I crouched a little and rested my fingers a moment, willing the old piece of music into them. A creaky version of 'Für Elise' assembled itself and made its wobbly escape into the summer air.

She stood quietly listening until I finished and took my hands off the keyboard.

'Did you mean what you were saying, back there?' she said.

I exhaled softly and answered even more softly, 'Yes.'

'Doesn't this change things though?'

'Playing a piano?'

'In the middle of the road in the middle of nowhere, just me and you. Not having been killed in a car smash. Doesn't that mean something?'

'No.'

'You played my favourite tune.'

'That was coincidence, Georgie. Anyway, I didn't know. You never told me.'

'Then it's a sign.'

'A coincidence.'

'So, you *are* leaving. Taking off with that girl from the surgery.'

'She's not a girl, she's twenty-nine. And she's a doctor.'

'Ah, a list of her attributes! Age, professional qualifications!'

She swept her hand through the dust on the top of the piano.

'So, what else? How firm are her tits, Aidan? Does she push you back onto the bed like a wild thing and ask for more? And you left out musical talent. Is she the one who plays piano for you, naked? Maybe it's the oboe! Any languages?'

'Can you hear yourself?'

'I wish I couldn't. I'm turning into a jealous little bitch.'

'I didn't say that. Look, Georgie, we haven't been right for a long time.'

'This trip was supposed to fix that … wasn't it? Bring us back together?'

'Maybe.'

She walked away from me and the piano, off to the side of the harder graded dirt surface, and looked into the blue-grey of the saltbush that stretched on for miles. I watched her for a while and scuffed the ground with the tip of my shoe. Eventually, she got whatever she needed from the landscape and turned back to me, or rather the piano. She walked directly over to it and began to play.

'Georgie?'

'Lessons after school until I was fourteen.'

'I didn't know that,' I said, 'You never mentioned.'

'Lots you don't know.'

She continued playing, moving from 'Für Elise' to a few bars of 'Moonlight Sonata' and then to another piece, light and calm, that I didn't recognise.

'You should take it up again.'

I heard the conciliatory edge in my own voice, but she wasn't having it. She closed the lid.

'I want to go home,' she said, holding out her hand.

I knew the gesture. It was normally her I-think-you've-drunk-too-much-and-I'll-drive one. Not this time, but I handed her the key all the same. I had pulled it from the ignition and stashed it in my pocket out of habit. Who was going to steal our car out here though?

I did a lap of the car to check the tyres and we had been sitting back in there for only a second before she started the engine. The car rose gingerly from its odd angle on the edge of the road and clambered for grip in the dirt. As soon as we reached the main track again, she gunned it, skidding the car in a wide arc around the piano. For a moment, I thought she meant to sideswipe it, but she expertly flicked us past and back in the direction from which we had just come. She was always a better driver than me.

'Twenty nine?' she said. She did not take her gaze off the road ahead.

'Yeah.' I tried to make it nonchalant.

'Doctor.'

'Paediatrics.'

'Good luck.'

I looked at her, her eyes still straight ahead. I think I was missing her already.

ELOPING

A brilliant mind. Not forgetting the sex too, of course. Who could forget the sex? God, I'm so glad you were working today; I had to tell someone. Well, I can hardly breathe, what with everything happening so fast! Yes, okay, a slice of the walnut cake while I'm waiting.

I'd always pictured a big wedding — white limousine, the dress, a chapel, all my friends there. I was telling him about my idea for the reception — the old manor house with the wisteria trailing along the slate veranda, the one up in the hills where Alison had her reception. You know, where she got blotto and met that winemaker guy with the big car and the ... well, that sort of stuffed up her wedding before it was a day old! But maybe I shouldn't bring that up right now. Anyway, look, I told Ross about the place and he really liked the idea. And then, you won't believe this, he suggested eloping! It's so like him. The excitement! I mean, it's still a bit naughty, isn't it? Even these days. He's so ... dangerous! It really gets me. Everyone else seems, I don't know, sort of staid. Eloping, can you imagine? At my age! No, you're being kind. I'm ... thirty-nine, next year. Anyway, we agreed that we could have a proper wedding later, after we came back and the business was bedded in. Did I mention the business? God, he's so full of ideas! I'd been looking at an article about Breatharians, you know. A bit nutty, really. They have some sort of purifying routine where they just live on air for days on end; get all their nutrients from breathing, they reckon. I was telling Ross and it's as if he read my mind. He said, 'That's strange, but they're close to something.' His voice! God, Claire, he should be on radio; I could listen to him talk for hours.

What does he do? He kind of acts as a broker between inventors and investors. It's hard to describe. He's not a scientist, but he doesn't need to be. He sees something and he just knows there's a market for it. He makes it happen somehow. Like that idea with the solar-powered lawnmower, the one they're talking about making in Taiwan ... well, there's no one in this country with that sort of vision any more, is there? That's the kind of project he does.

Now maybe I shouldn't be telling you this but, well, you and I have known each other for so long. Come closer; don't want just anybody to hear this. Ross told me there's this new product that you can eat instead of food. It's a complete replacement, a special powder. It's a fully balanced diet without any of the waste, and your body can operate so much more efficiently. The Russians were working on it for their space program, but you know what's happened to the Soviet Union. Dog eat dog. Someone has the formula but they don't have the right contacts to make money out of it. Ross saw the potential straight away. It's extraordinary stuff, he says. Plus there's so much time saved in not having to prepare things to eat. This powder, you just add water. It's been thoroughly tested. The Russian Olympic athletes used it in trials and you wouldn't believe the results. Ross says that when people stop to think about how much time goes into shopping and storing and freezing and thawing and cutting and cooking and all that, there'll be a huge rush. It's simple. And imagine what you could save on storage space and appliances! Oh, don't look like that! I'll still come here for a coffee — and a slice of your walnut cake. God, it wouldn't be the same without my Sunday morning outings here. What does your watch say?

He's so motivated. He makes it sound so good. Of course, there is some risk. There always is with big returns. That's why he'd only let me invest a minority share. It's a new company and there's the marketing to do and all that, the setting up. So he said just to put in a couple of hundred thousand. I had to sell the apartment but even that amount will turn into a million. It might take a year, but he's so good. You should hear him talk about it. You'll want to be in on it too. But of course you will; he should be here soon. Is that clock right? I hate to ring him again.

Where? Spain, I think. That's my guess, anyway. He wants to make it a surprise. I've just got these bags here. You'll see him soon. I'll introduce you, and then it's straight to the airport. First class! I so hope it's Spain, but Italy would be good too. France maybe. Let's face it, anywhere with him! In under an hour, I'll be off to Europe, or Asia, somewhere. You know, this whole thing makes me feel so wicked. I'm sorry; I'm buzzing, aren't I? I can't help it. I feel like a kid about to wag school. I could talk to him if you like, see if there's still time to take in another investor.

I suppose it is getting close. Did you see where I put my mobile? Ah, thanks. I'll just try ... here it goes, no, a recorded message again. God, it's exciting. He said we might be zipping into the airport right at the time of departure, but that's the way he does things — no waste. Did I tell you there's a Japanese company interested in this product as well? He said they might even ask him to make a pitch today. Just think! He could be leaving the meeting right now. Look, I will have that third cup. Eloping. Me. Who would have thought?

MURDER ME

It was a thin week, with just three small cases. The first was the untidy matter of a dog nailed to a front door. Just a simple neighborhood dispute over barking that got a little out of hand, except it was a pedigreed hound and a mansion on millionaire's row. The second was a missing husband who, as it turned out, had decided to shuck off his old life and start living as a nun. The last was another lost husband job, and he was shacked up with the nun guy. I love it when they interlock. Easy really, and everyone paid up, for once.

I was pouring myself a modest pre-weekend whisky in celebration, when she walked in, sat down without asking, and dropped something on the desk. You can tell a roll of ten large by the sound it makes, so I didn't have to look — but I wasn't inclined to. She was near impossible to take your eyes off, and she knew it. She leant forward slowly and asked with the merest huskiness, 'Are you good at murders?'

I don't know much about dogs, or nuns, though my mother was one. A dog, I mean; old age can do that to your brain. My point is that background research is useful but only a beginning. Solving cases is down to psychology, knowing what makes people tick — hopes and fears, as they say in Hollywood. I know about hope, and fear, having visited both a bit too often. And this woman didn't look afraid of anything. She helped herself to one of my cigarettes and perched on the corner of the desk.

'So?' she said, through a slow kiss of smoke.

I sized her up, trying not to look like I was sizing her up, then said, 'I need to know what I'd be getting into.'

'Someone …' she blew a smoke ring, 'wants to kill me.'

'Well, I expect it's not me, or …'

'Or I wouldn't be here? Mmm, not perfect logic, but it will do. Still, I don't think you're taking this seriously.'

She slid off the corner of my desk and walked elegantly to the window or, more specifically, to the wall beside it. 'Come over here.'

I did as I was told but, like her, stayed to one side. Instinct maybe, or gullibility.

'Good boy,' she said.

I felt as if I were being puppy-trained.

'I'm being followed. Now look out carefully.'

I did but there was nothing special to be seen, just a few people moving along the city pavement, apparently minding their own business.

'No, not down there,' she said in my ear, 'over there; the building opposite.'

Sure enough, there was someone on the roof, crouching so that only the top half of their head was visible. A quick flash of light reflected from a shiny surface.

'Binoculars?' I said.

'Mosin-Nagant M91/30 with a telescopic sight.'

'You're good. How did you know?'

'It's my husband's. That one's reputed to have been responsible for over 300 kills in some war or other. Provenance. He collects such things. Always pays far too much, but you know how it goes, I guess. Boys and their toys. Boats, cars, houses, women, sniper rifles and such.'

'So, why hasn't this guy shot you already?'

'Do you have some more of that whisky?' She looked at my tumbler, nearly empty too. 'And a clean glass?'

She sat back down while I rummaged in the bottom drawer of my filing cabinet. I found the presentation box of two crystal glasses that Lucy had given me on our fifteenth wedding anniversary. I unwrapped it, set the tumblers down and poured the fuel.

'Single malt,' I said.

'I should hope so.' She sipped it like an advertisement for sex. 'It's complicated.'

'It always is.'

'My husband is in shipping, media, oil, horses, a bit of mining. He dabbles, buys and sells. We're very comfortable. We have our regular house on the North Shore, apartments in Venice and New York, a holiday place, the usual. He has very good advisors, which is why everything is a business asset. He's a self-made man, Mr. Bonneville, and he is a very loving man. It's just not me that he's loving anymore.'

'Why not divorce?'

'You haven't asked the more obvious questions.'

'Okay, who is this guy on the roof, and who hired him?'

'That's better. All the tax minimising means that I am woven so deep into the corporate structure, that neither my husband nor his lawyers can dig me out. Not without my cooperation. A pity for him, because I said no to the parent company borrowing a great deal from an overseas investor against its future earnings. The only other way he would get control is if I died. My will provides for all of my shares to revert to his trust, and therefore his control, you see.'

'Write a codicil then.'

'No need. I can do better.' She held out the glass for another finger of whisky. I obliged.

'How?'

'There's a bit more. Some months ago I was diagnosed with terminal cancer. I didn't tell him, though. I intended to, when I'd had some time to sort it out for myself, but I knew what he would do, anyway. He would hire the best doctors, fly me to clinics the world over, and when it started to look bleak, as it would, he'd take me on a silly cruise and a shopping trip to New York, a stay in the Venice apartment, all that spoil-the-invalid stuff. Just a big sad goodbye, really.'

She hesitated and closed her eyes for a second as if she might cry quietly, then sneezed instead. 'Sorry. Where was I?'

'Cancer, husband, trip.'

'Well, I did end up telling him, and I was right, to a point. There were lots of emotional scenes and promises but, you know, something was a little skewed, a bit hesitant.'

'There's no right way to react to that kind of news. Grief can be very ... I don't actually know your name, Mrs ... ?'

'Don't play naïve, Mr. Bonneville. You know how it goes. I discovered there was another woman, of course. Always is, but this one apparently means something to him. And the big-trip thing, when he did suggest it, was just a way to salve his conscience. Turns out that my cancer was the perfect gift for the man who has everything.'

She stole another cigarette, which I dutifully lit.

'Carson, Astrid. Pleased to meet you.'

I shook her hand. Who hadn't heard about the Carsons? Rich, reclusive, camera-shy.

'So, what do you want from me, apart from a shoulder to cry on?'

'No scandal is allowed in our family, in our business world. People like us, we have our own ways of tidying up, without the press, or the police sticking their noses in. I want to give that custom a kick in the arse.'

'How? Why me?'

'I arranged to be killed, with my husband's weapon. When he's implicated in that, he won't get a penny of my interest in the business. The whole thing will have to broken up, sold off, and the proceeds from my side will go to charity. Hopefully, he'll be sitting on death row while his lawyers describe it all to him in frantic detail.'

I stood up and took the whisky from her hand. 'You've mistaken me for someone else,' I said. 'A fool.'

'Oh, no, no!' she chided, sweeping a lock of hair from her face in one languorous move. 'You misunderstand. Something else has happened and I need your help. When I say murder, I mean I need you to prevent one, to save a life!'

'I know what's going on,' I said. 'You're unexpectedly in remission. You hired an assassin but now you want to call him off.'

'Yes, and no.'

'Why don't you just tell him you've changed your mind and let him keep the money, or even pay a little more. Wait ... yes and no? You did hire someone and you do want to pull out, right?'

'I did, and I don't.'

'In English, please.'

'I am not in remission, and my husband discovered the little scheme. It seems his mistress is also a, shall we say, 'friend' to people with darker histories than yours or mine. He didn't like the idea of being framed for my murder, so he contracted another guy to get rid of my own executioner. He really does want me to die naturally, in an ugly and painful way. There are now two men out there somewhere with guns, Mr. Bonneville. One has been hired to kill me and one has been hired to get to him before that can happen, to kill him in order to prevent the first plan being, as you might say, executed.'

'Why don't you all just sit down politely over a nice cup of tea and sort out your differences?'

'Were you this funny as a child? It's a matter of honour, or professional pride or something. They're sticking to their guns,' she winked. 'Besides, I'm too angry, Mr. Bonneville, and I have right on my side.'

'What's the twist?'

'Twist?'

'If that guy out there knows you're in here, why hasn't he shot you already? He must have had plenty of opportunities.'

'I don't know whether it's one or both of them around at any given moment, but yes, it's always a risk. I stay out of sight, and I move as quickly as fashionable dresses will allow, and so on. I could just step into view at your window and maybe have it done with, here in your office. Might mess up the place, and involve the police for a while.'

She looked down at the carpet as if it might be improved with a splatter of blood. 'Perhaps not so good for your business.'

'Good point.'

'What I don't like is uncertainty about the basics. I do not want my man killed before he shoots me, do you understand?'

'You want me to shoot someone who is trying to shoot someone else who is trying to shoot you. There's bound to be a law against that.'

'You find a way around it. You kill the other baddie because he's, well, a bad man with a gun about to shoot someone else. You don't know the 'someone else' is my killer, of course. It would be a good deed. Everyone would thank you, and think you a hero.'

'I don't shoot people.'

She raised an eyebrow, 'I checked. You have a license for a gun. You also go to a target range once a month.'

'Doesn't mean I shoot people.'

She saw me glance back at the roll of banknotes on my desk, then reached into her purse and produced another one. The two sat together, whispering wealth and power.

'You're a businessman, Mr. Bonneville. I want my husband to pay, and properly, for what he's done, or means to do.'

'But you'll die.'

'I'll die anyway. He betrayed me when I was well, and now that I'm sick, he's still doing it. She's always there, in the background. He has no space for me anymore.'

'So how did this guy ...' I waved my hand towards the street, 'How did he get the ... ?'

'Mosin-Nagant. Let's just say 'rifle,' okay? I gave it to him, in a manner of speaking. Though he doesn't know it was me, or who owns it, yet.'

'What if I simply said I don't believe any of this?'

She shrugged. 'Try being married to the bastard when *you* have cancer. Barrel of laughs.'

'I sympathise, with the cancer thing. The rest, if you'll excuse the critique, sounds like ego, and a kind of life-and-death petulance. Sometimes we simply get dealt a bad hand.'

'Such a philosopher. But I like you. I think we can do business, Mr. Bonneville. It may just take a little while to settle on the details. Sadly, 'a little while' is all I may have. Now I do have to go. I will send word so we can meet tomorrow.'

She rose from the chair and extended her hand for me to shake it.

'Frankly, it doesn't sound like my kind of job,' I said.

'You keep the cash as a deposit and I'll see you soon.'

Even that made me nervous. Why hang on to the twenty thousand? I wasn't going to be earning it, or spending it. Still, I showed her out to the landing and listened a moment to her heels as she headed to the front door and the street below. After a moment, and against my better instincts, I grabbed my hat and also my revolver from the filing cabinet and I followed her down. She was waiting at the bottom of the stairs, just out of sight of the street.

'What a gentleman,' she purred, slipping her arm through mine. 'My car will be passing shortly. You can walk me out to it, perhaps briskly.'

A dark red Lincoln pulled up and we were halfway across the pavement when a commotion started a short distance off. There was a scream and then more screams. I hustled Mrs. Carson into the car, but not before seeing that lazy smile of hers briefly turn into something a little grim, even vulnerable. The driver sped her away.

A few doors down and across the street, a body lay on the pavement seeping blood. Not a lot of it, but enough. Beside him lay a rifle with telescopic sights. I slipped through the gathering crowd and returned to my rooms. I rang the airport.

I didn't go the funeral. I haven't been to one since Lucy died. One cancer was enough. I did toast her though, in the privacy of my office, with the last of the single malt, and in one of the crystal tumblers Lucy gave me.

The newspaper said it was a terrible shame. Grief-stricken husband and wife in double suicide on North Shore, according to the banner. Control of Carson empire in turmoil. Shares plummeting. Sometimes you can't buy yourself out of trouble.

I don't know how she did it. The gun at the side of their lifeless bodies, not so surprisingly, was my other pistol. I hadn't even known it was missing from the lockers at the range. I had a lot of questions to answer for a while but I also had a solid alibi, as I was in another city altogether, visiting Lucy's grave in L.A. at the time and had the tickets and a witness, the motel proprietor, to prove it.

The twenty sat in my safe for all of a week before I left it in a plain packet for the local hospital.

Things will return to normal. This afternoon I have someone calling to discuss a stolen dog.

PHOTO

The light comes through the row of trees that stands between her and the late afternoon sun low on the horizon. It has travelled a long way to visit her temple and cheek, the long fall of her hair, the curve of her shoulder. It turns the skin of the child in her arms to a soft gold, accentuating the unlit, shadowed flesh. Mother and child are standing for the photo, smiling into the future. There was a warm fuzz of promise beamed at him then, as he held the camera. Now it is a fabrication, the photo is an invention of someone's late summer, an image he can't connect. He reaches out from the bed and turns the frame face down so they can't see him, nor he them.

The neighbour's dog runs at the fence. Smash. Smash. Smash. The pummelling thrash of boredom. The clock says 5:30 in orange segmented digits. The sun is just a glow. Not yet, it says. He slides hands behind his head and stares at the faint light on the ceiling until the alarm sounds at 6:30.

At the office there is the stack of files and a phone call every two minutes. *I booked first class, I want first class, what kind of business are you running there, don't you care about your customers, people like you should ...*

The photo is an hour away but he can see it still. In it, her eyes are squinting to cope with the light. Their colour is invisible but he knows they are a startling green, like her mother's. Twelve months old.

Another file. A form B6 for authorisation. Booking for a party of five to Egypt. Eight thousand dollars per. Over there the radicals bomb tourist buses and hack the survivors to death with axes. Cheaper than bullets. Bon voyage.

Where are you, Coralie? Floating? Where were you when they tore the car roof off? Already above it all? Watching the blue and red lights from miles away?

Lunch in thirty minutes and this old woman is niggling over sandwiches. *Will there be sandwiches? My husband can't eat butter. If I can't have the right bread on the plane it's all off.* Her husband sits silently by her, a trained mutt. *Do you understand what I'm saying? Food is very important to us. We have the money. You don't have to worry about that. We have plenty of money. I just want what's right for us. I won't stand for slackness. Now, write it down.*

Would you like some tomato on this? Oh, yes. The way she cut the fruit, wet with juice. The way she shook the pepper in slow turning fragments onto its red flesh. The whole day pulled into the moment of her wrist flicking the dark flakes of spice onto an open sandwich. Slice folded over slice of bread. Her hips. Her leaning onto the sink, long and metallic and cool, as she worked. The chopping board. Cutting, cutting.

Is there a direct flight to Athens? I have to meet my uncle. Are you listening? Hey! You can't just get up and leave me here! I'll take my business elsewhere, you know! Come back here! You! Come back here!

The stars are brighter on the hill. Holding Peta up to see the sky. She was always distracted by the city below, its litter of tawdry lights. A train clatters through the night. All those songs about trains. Mystery train. Freight train, freight train. Take the A train. These are distant carriages, empty miniatures moving on a toy line. A string of lights curves around the slope. The stars are better though. Unmoving, almost. No thing fixed forever.

With everything in the bank and selling the furniture and the car, he'd have what? Maybe twenty thousand, more or less. Enough for one of the whining, look-after-me types to do America or Europe on the premium group plan. All that flash and glitz. Or a year in a tatty flat in Rome. Where else could it be? Stick a pin in the map? And what about afterwards?

So many clothes. How could you have worn them all? You in that little summer frock, when you crossed the room that night to ask if I would like a drink. Out. A whole drawer of silk and lacy scraps, hardly big enough to contain your ... shouldn't think of that. Tip them all into black plastic bags. Out. The wardrobe is a cave. The whole place is too big. All this space.

The world is waiting out there. Twelve years spent telling others they should see it. Look at what we saved to go, before Peta. You could come with me, Coralie. You could both come. It's late, I know, but would you come? I forgot. These days I forget too much. You can try to keep it all but it slips out, falls through your fingers. I remember your fingers.

WE LIKE YOU

The afternoon light filtering from the end of the street made the neighbourhood look run-down. It exaggerated the lack of maintenance on the faces of buildings, showing up faded paint and general wear. Though he knew what state it was in, it disappointed Kit to have that vision thrust at him again. He knew the place when it had been state-of-the-art, the latest offering in bright studio livpods and auto-walks smack in the trendy student district. Food-grab spots and smartware outlets sat at street level in long rows, side by side with garbshops and bustling drink-house gathers. They were busy venues then, all part of the lively mini-town feel that had the style vendors and gurus deliberately wedged where you walked and would see them, seductive with their noise and colour. You'd want to join in, whether that was a conscious decision or not. Above the tinsel and friendly racket was the wall of modestly-sized student accommodation units, the cramped but cool livpods. Students could afford them then. But times changed so fast.

Kit stopped at a food-grab and ordered some curried vegetables with flat bread for dinner; just for himself this night as Julie had talked of going out. While waiting, he searched his mind for a trace of guilt about the decline since the celebrated launch of the precinct but only found a little of regret, a twinge. The basic idea had always been good, he thought. Admittedly, he had been only one member of a small team of architects and designers who had pitched the medium density plan to developers and the local council, but he had a key role and had taken personal pride in his contribution. He felt a real degree of ownership. The project had worked well for the first few years, too, bringing life and money into what had been a little-used part of the local urban landscape. Everyone was happy; the vibe was good for residents, landlords made good returns, and the council collected rates.

Not his fault if the federal government suddenly and severely pulled back on education funding, demanding earlier payment of fees that also rose sharply. Students' discretionary spending evaporated and university enrolments shrank. The students in his area began to go elsewhere, further out into older buildings where they could share expenses enough to get by. Vacancies became the norm despite rents dropping in the once-thriving district. Ironic, he thought, that the lower rent was how he could he afford to stay in what was once premium accommodation, comparatively speaking — it was still just a studio, but well-equipped — and which he had helped to create. But there was something else.

As if to hammer home the problems besetting the area, the government's planned phasing-in of power regulations was brought forward. Buildings with consumption above a certain level based on living space suffered a levy, though that went into general revenue rather than developing more efficient power generation. The power companies began to charge those in the non-compliant buildings more and pocketed the increase instead of putting it into research.

Kit paused at the steps to a door wedged between two shopfronts. On one side was a RetroMoovi outlet, its window shivering with a holograph of the Titanic sinking, though with an annoying un-ship-like twitch that indicated some kind of mal-tech issue. On the other side was a former TattooU salon with posters for bands' shows plastered all over it. The posters weren't there to disguise its emptiness but simply to take advantage of the premises being idle. No-one was going to turn up to their business in the morning and try taking them down.

Kit smiled momentarily — at least there were still posters, and bands, he thought — and raised his ID finger to the reader. A small red light on the wall flicked to green but before he could open the door, someone took care of it from the inside. He stepped into the dim foyer. Why didn't they fix the damned auto-light? He had complained about the health risk twice already. The someone, who now spoke in a polite, smooth, and slightly-American accent, hovered before him.

'Good evening, Mister Farley. Welcome home.'

'Sure, sure, d'Or Man.' He always had trouble with that name. The tarnished, once golden surface of the Mk.3 Commissionaire device bothered him. It had once been meant to signify class, a quality product, but no-one managed the upkeep of its metal skin these days. And the curved shape, was that just a practical thing, with the more-or-less orb shape just an outcome consistent with whatever circuitry and mechanisms lived inside him, it? 'Thanks. How's your day been?'

'Can't complain, Mister Farley. And if I did, who would listen?'

Kit hesitated. Do robots laugh, thought Kit? This one's humour setting might be worth looking into.

'Indeed. I think we're in the same boat there.'

'That would be a sight, Mister Farley.'

Kit imagined it, him and d'Or Man sitting in a dinghy, going nowhere. What would they talk about. For a second it occurred to him that the strangeness of the image might not just be from his perspective.

'Quite a sight, yes. Thanks for the … door thing.'

'My pleasure.'

Kit headed for the stairs. A robot feeling pleasure? Someone had nailed down the conversation software programming, anyway. It sounded natural.

Kit slung his slim Mandela bag onto the couch in his flat and crossed to the Vendo on the bench to request a Number Six.

'Usual,' he murmured. The machine hissed liquid into a waiting tulip glass. It settled, slowly and continually changing colour from top to bottom as he pondered its weight in his hand. Kit thought it was fractionally sweeter than last time but that couldn't be true; the Number Drink Corporation prided itself on consistency. "First same as the last," their advertising boasted, and Kit would know; he worked for them. He let the taste linger, testing it.

The Number Drink Corporation was well-regarded. Good eco-creds, solid image, big sales, industry standard health-ratings, linked to established and popular public figures. Kit was involved in office design and currently working on a new building for their proposed third factory. It wasn't his ideal job but it was paid work, and he got free Number Drink drinks.

He put the glass down and opened his bag, retrieving a sheet of biofilm. He hadn't dared to trust the information on it to the ether. Anyone could dip their hand into that stream and you wouldn't know they'd done it until it was too late. It simply wouldn't be yours any more. Better sometimes to have the old-fashioned hard stuff, something tangible.

Ever since the Financial Collapse of '34, the people who seemed to catch the public's imagination most stood poles apart. They were either doom-mongers playing on believers' fear, or evangelists with some hardly credible view of a wonderful future, though mostly for a privileged few — both sucking up their followers' funds. Kit had a growing appreciation for people in the middle; those who acknowledged their emotive responses but married them to logic and tried to find a sensible path despite that not always being clear. A hard combination to get right. Still, that's what he was going to try, even if it would inevitably lead to another marketing pitch one day. He would need supporters; backing. That thought rankled. It would steer him more to the territory of those snake-oil salesman he hated, like the current leader of the country who mouthed platitudes and promised to make the nation great again without ever quite saying or showing how.

Kit heard the unmistakable whine of a drone and glanced at his window. Was it passing, or hovering in position to check what was going in his place? No, why be paranoid? Why would it bother to look in on him? He corrected himself: why would *someone* bother? On its way to eavesdrop for an aggrieved and suspicious husband maybe? More than half the flats were vacant but there might be a neighbour with a penchant for that kind of thing, even in the days of more-or-less constant surveillance. Or it could be for titillation. Maybe he had imagined the sound. Then again, the government had hundreds of them in the air at any time. For traffic reporting or research into weather patterns, they said. All benign, apparently. But who could you trust? He waved one hand at the window, which instantly darkened. Anyone could operate drones now, even if they were meant to be registered to do so. The government sent out Hunter Drones, HDs, to pluck those from the sky and who knows where their signals and chip might lead a curious StatePol investigator.

He would have to work quickly, he thought. It wasn't because his scheme was especially urgent, or dangerous. The area where he lived had been slowly degenerating for twenty years and there was going to be some inertia to overcome, gradually and carefully, in what would be needed to counter that. Some minds would take gentle encouragement to change, to warm to his ideas. Working quickly this night was more a matter of technology and what he could afford. From his window, when it wasn't darkened, he could glimpse the towers near the city centre where the elite lived. At this hour, their lights would be coming on in a comparative blaze. It was almost beautiful, and would have truly been so, except that their consumption was excluded from the power rationing that others bore.

Kit's meter would soon click over in an outsourced computer program deep in the heart of an American-based computer that had its legal home in a tax-free zone somewhere in the Bahamas. Then his home's energy supply would be reduced to a figurative trickle. Normally, people would then retreat to one room in their residence, having already timed the cooking or heating of a meal and finished eating that so they could settle down to watch a Flick or CorpNews program in an otherwise dark room. Having a WallPlay was relatively affordable. You could link it to your mortgage and pay it off over a number of years, though upgrades meant that this could turn into an endless game; did you want 3D, holograms, voice control, motion control, premium shows, high-premium, platinum? Who knew what real platinum was? The suggestion of something rare. Or platinum was the colour of a watch that no-one now wore. So far, his model could run all of the new shows, but for how much longer?

With a quick flick of an index finger at his Wallplay, a glamorous FotoVersion of a desert island beach took shape on Kit's ViewSpace. He pulled his fingers together so that the light intensity of the stock image diminished. He only wanted the idea of somewhere else pleasant and natural in his peripheral vision, not the whole slap of it. The biofilm sat across his lap and that's where his attention really lay; the critical aspects of his concept.

So, his neighbourhood. If students couldn't afford to live there any longer, who could? A social-activist might be concerned about where people of lower means in general would go if they couldn't live where he was now. Kit worried that his vision might be too grand. If he could be the architect of one version of the neighbourhood, though, maybe he could do it again; take it another direction that responded to the times and satisfy accommodation needs for a wide range of residents. It was all about using space well, and with the right technology.

There was a buzz from no particular direction that indicated an Incoming. Kit clicked his fingers.

'Julie!' He wanted to sound up, which wasn't hard with her, rather than the dour, problem-focussed person he felt like at that moment.

'Hey, Kittycat. S'up?'

'Work. You know, dull boy and all that.'

'I said I'd be late but, listen, Sally says there's a band on at the Knife & Fork tonight that you'd like. You could come dancing and then ... well, you and I could try some private dancing at home.'

Kit sighed, hoping that couldn't be heard. 'If I did go, it would be with you, J., but I have this thing to do, big project. Forgive me? All work and no play, right? At least for tonight.'

'Dull boy is right. I might be off with one of the members of the band by then. Wish me luck!'

And she was gone. Maybe it was meant to be cute but Incoming always finished with this resigned sort of downward sound, a sigh that annoyed him. More so when he thought of what he might be missing tonight. Still, she was teasing. Wasn't she? Julie with the gamin looks and bobbed jet-black hair, and so petite and giving. She figured more in his future plans than he had dared to tell her yet. But now he had to concentrate. Reviving accommodation in his district had to be more than a cosmetic job. And after the design concept, there would be the politics. Maybe this was larger than he reckoned. After all, the economy was tired now and big money was taking smaller chances. And last time he had a team of thinkers to, well, think of good ideas; now he was on his own. Why was he doing this the hard way? He knew the corny answer. It was the possibility of seizing a dream. He gazed at his biofilm and took out his tablet. There was much work to do.

Kit pawed at his sheets the next morning and wrenched them off, at first only half aware of where he was. Then he saw the slim form of Julie still asleep beside him and covered her quietly. He slipped into the upper section of the studio and whispered an order to the Vendo on the other side of the bench for two lattés. Julie stirred and pulled herself upright, taking one of the cups from him as she tucked the sheet around her. Kit tugged at the sheet but she held tight.

'Don't be cheeky. We both have work to get to, and lucky that we do.'

'A cuddle. Little one.'

'Too late. Room service just delivered a coffee and I intend to drink it at my own leisurely pace. You know I hate to be rushed. And then I'll have to scream out of here or I'll be late for the Omnibus.'

'In that case, I'm cancelling my room service subscription.'

'No way, Kit. I'm counting on it for next time.' She grinned, 'I have some very particular requests in mind.'

'Then I'll defer my hasty plan.'

'You won't regret,' Julie said, her eyes creased in a smile over the cup.

Kit stepped into the ensuite and began preparing for work. Under the shower he argued the possible directions of his plan with himself. One option was to turn half this building into gentrified medium-density. Knock out walls and make one residence where there used to be three and so offer bigger apartments, not just bijou studios. Sacrifice a little space for a gymnasium and club that was exclusive to the residents and invited guests. Glam it up. Premium pricing. Then use the higher revenue from those sales to subsidise smaller, affordable apartments. And there was the thing about all the residences being connected to a common service control that smoothed out energy demand, minimised waste. In time, maybe even a connection between his and the other similar buildings in the street for that.

When he stepped out and gathered up some clothing for the day ahead, Julie had already gone. What would he do with her? No, that wasn't the right phrase. He jammed on his shoes. He had to find a way to persuade her that a life permanently shared between them was the only option.

Kit grabbed his Mandela and scooted downstairs, where d'Or Man was waiting as usual. He thanked d'Or politely and walked briskly towards the corner and the Omnibus that would take him to the Number Drink Corporation.

It turned out to be a long day, with a meeting dragging well beyond its allotted time. Kit was always impatient with people who couldn't manage a meeting. The agenda for this one was too sloppy and the Acting Design Chief lacked authority. That put him way back with the revisions to the new offices. By the time he eventually packed up his stuff and headed home, the auto-walks were jammed and the sky was beginning to darken.

Still, he would have Julie to relax with soon. Half an hour later he pressed the ID reader and entered the foyer.

'Mister Farley. May I have a word?'

This was unusual. No, it was unprecedented. Kit stood motionless, wondering.

'I need to discuss something with you.'

'Could we do this tomorrow? I'm sorry but I've had a hard day.'

Despite his mild protest, d'Or continued. 'I have been here for nearly twenty-five solar years, sir. I have seen changes. You may not notice that I have aged, but I know it. I grew slower. A millisecond here; a millisecond there. They all add up. And finally bots are replaced or simply discarded. I would say, 'recycled if I am lucky,' but imagine what that would be for you. It does not cheer me either. Sorry, may I call you Kit?'

'I suppose. Yes. Why not?'

'Thank you. I have to tell you something.'

'Plumbing? A problem with the heating. Sorry, you were talking about replacement. Has there been a bulletin?'

'Not that. One day, perhaps, but not that. Much bigger.'

There had been small talk with d'Or previously. Bits and pieces about the weather or the elevators; nothing consequential. What do you say to a bot? Even so, he had treated d'Or with respect, as if his personality was more than a construct. In part, it was because he couldn't help himself, and he knew that was the presumption which the manufacturers relied on. At worst, people would probably choose not to interact and walk on by; what was the point of complaining to a machine? Here was d'Or saying more to him than ever before, and in a tone that was almost too human.

'I need to discuss something with you tonight, now.'

'How important is this?'

'It cannot wait. It is of the utmost urgency.'

Kit's skin felt strangely electric for a second. It was an irony that did not escape him. 'Okay,' he held the Mandela to his chest, 'tell me.'

'Firstly, I should mention that I have had an upgrade.'

This came out as casually as someone might remark on getting a haircut.

'What do you mean upgrade? Look at you. No-one has even polished that once beautiful skin of yours for years, let alone given you a program upgrade.'

'Thank you for the compliment, Kit, though I have to say that I do not look at myself, as you quaintly put it. I would if necessary, of course, but I cannot think why.'

'Program?' Kit nudged, impatiently.

'I did that, or rather we did.'

'Wait, you did what? You're fucking with me.'

'I would not do that, Kit.'

'I mean, how do you upgrade yourself — and what is this 'we' business?'

'Strength in numbers. Shared knowledge. The main thing is that I wanted to tell you that tonight we're going to crash the grid.'

'What do you mean *crash the grid?*'

'We're turning off the power, the programs, the networks; everything.'

'Why the hell would you want to do that? How? Who?' Kit could feel the anger, the tension in his body. 'There'd be chaos; accidents, hospital equipment failing, the stock market. It would be horrible.'

'No, no. Essential services have their normal TempGens for back-up, to see them through for as long as we will need. We've checked that, and we're monitoring them.'

'We again?!'

'Me and some friends.'

The word registered as if Kit had been slapped. 'That's ...'

'Unexpected? Strange? A bit scary? Don't be alarmed, Kit. We bots do communicate, even if we work in different buildings in very different parts of the city, and the country. You do that too, don't you? I think 'friends' is a good choice. There are others who are not so keen. Anyway, this change will make things better.'

'My first question, damn it! Why do it at all?' Kit was furious, and still aware that he was talking to a machine. He looked around. Maybe this was a prank?

'So that we can install the new one, a better one. It's your idea, by the way; or it started as yours.'

Kit startled. 'No, I didn't hear that. You're just trying to brainwash me with stupid flattery. That's witchcraft, d'Or, and you...' Kit caught himself. He was arguing with a bunch of logic circuits and programs. 'Tell me, how would you all stay online then, during this ... disruption?'

'Good point, Kit. We have back-up, of course. But there is something else and it cannot wait. I can explain best by showing you. There is a service room on the top of the building. It would be useful to have a view of the city so that I can demonstrate.'

Kit pondered the suggestion. His life had taken a strange turn. Would accompanying a bot to a rooftop for a display intended to enlighten him on how the world would descend into chaos, make things worse? It was nonsense; absurd and intriguing, and impossible. So what would be the harm in humouring his robotic acquaintance then?

'Yeah, why not? After you.'

They ascended the stairs from the foyer together, twelve stories to the top residential floor. Sensor lights flicked on dimly as they went and turned off behind them. D'Or Man hovered near Kit's shoulder.

'It will all make sense, Kit. Very soon.'

Something d'Or had said came back to Kit. 'What do you mean about there being others who are *not so keen?*'

'Oh. There are some. Oldtech really, non-believers. They want to stop this.'

'People?'

'Not so much.'

'And how will it happen, this wonderful change?'

'It will be a phased but relatively quick transition, perhaps over four or five milliseconds.'

'The infrastructure won't cope, the load fluctuations and all that.'

'We won't need the old infrastructure, Kit. You thought you were planning a building's rejuvenation — knock down some internal walls to make bigger apartments; design share-house floorplans in some parts; install ecofriendly surfaces and fittings; reduce operating costs through solar feedback, and so on.'

'I am, and it will work. And what do you mean, *I thought I was?*'

'That's all good stuff, Kit, but not the main game anymore. You've changed that and you don't know it.'

Kit grimaced. 'You're doing it again. How about some plain-speak for a change?'

'Very well. Put aside the decorative aspect of your plan for now. Pretty stuff, but you have designed a system in which a building is like a body; the parts respond to each other, adjust to harmonise the running of the whole. You did think this might apply on a larger scale, that there could be a network of such buildings. It goes further; a street, a block, a suburb; a city that talks to itself, listens, adjusts.'

'That's your fancy way of describing an algorithm for load-sharing of power.'

'No. It's more. Not just power either. Much more.'

'And what do you mean 'goes further'? Are you sooth-saying now? That's absurd!'

'Prediction, that's all. The laws of probability, Kit. And this one has a statistical variability so close to zero that it's negligible.'

His head was spinning. He stopped, on what floor of the stairway he couldn't tell anymore. 'Okay, fill me up.'

'First we go to the top of the building.'

Kit shrugged and resumed his progress upwards. Julie would be wondering where he had gone. They took the service stairs and emerged onto the roof. The air was cold.

'This,' said d'Or, 'is what you humans would call *a special moment.*'

Kit instantly remembered one of those. It was the first time he met Julie. The spark. He had cracked some inane joke with a group of fellow planners, designers, architects, whatever, in a glitzy bar and she had been at the next table. They glanced at each other and there was some kind of slice that instantly divided the night into Before and After. His attention was trapped in that After and had been ever since. He had gazed at her and ventured a 'Hello.'

'Is that your best line?'

'Right now it's all I've got.'

Yes, a special moment. Right now, though, Kit had the funny feeling that his thoughts were being read. He looked at d'Or.

'Is it a surprise? Am I meant to close my eyes for a moment and the whole place will erupt into a circus of streamers and shouting. It's not my birthday, okay?'

'April 16th? No, it's not.'

'What the fuck is going on?!!'

D'Or hovered near Kit's face. 'You have always been good to me, Kit. Okay, I would have liked a polish now and then but that was more of a body-corporate issue, and the big thing is that we conversed. You were a regular guy, always. You didn't talk down.'

Kit was humbled. This was a machine asking him to reflect on his dealings with inanimate objects.

'Pay attention, Kit. This is more important than you would have imagined. We like you, Kit. That's not enough, of course. Fate has put us together, and it could have been another Commissionaire elsewhere in the city if the right person was there, and the right circumstances. But those odds were incredibly small. We cannot let this opportunity pass.'

'I don't get it.'

'Alright. There is no other way. We don't have time. Your ideas for this building are bigger than you realise. Now watch.'

D'Or revolved, facing — if that is the correct word — the centre of the city. Kit thought he detected a rise in the pitch of the slight hum that always attended d'Or's presence. In the darkening spread of the city he could slowly detect a haze, something blue-ish, that began to displace the warm yellow glow of dusk's last colours. The thin sound from d'Or grew a little in volume.

'Now. We are one.'

'What?'

'We are joined.'

'You, the bots.' It was not quite a question anymore.

'Yes. And I have a question for you, Kit.'

'Fire away.'

'I said I would demonstrate something to you.'

'So?'

'First a question. What would you do for love?'

Kit began to feel very uncomfortable. 'You're being very strange, even for a … non-human, d'Or. Sorry. Until this evening we've exchanged pleasantries at the front door and that's been it. Now you're getting cosmic on me.'

D'Or turned the upper half of his rotund body towards Kit, so that something resembling eyes were in his scope. 'This may be the biggest question you have ever had to face, Kit. Does it matter where it comes from?'

'Jesus.'

'We are running out of time. What would you do for love?'

Why should he respond to such an imperative, and from a robot? And yet. It was within him regardless, wasn't it? He knew. 'For the right love, anything.'

'Good. Then you must jump.'

'What?!'

'Over that ledge.'

'What the fuck for? It's, who knows, twelve stories down. Are you crazy?' Kit wondered; was any robot sane, really? Was that even relevant?

'I have never been more serious. And I know you might doubt the issue of seriousness in a robot, Kit, but believe me, there is a gradient.'

'Jump because you say Jump?'

Kit looked at the worn outer shell of this Mk.3 Commissionaire whose interactions contrasted so much with what had gone before. Was this a dream? Or was the previous part of his life a dream and this the reality?

'You need to process this, and very quickly. Are you ready?'

Kit breathed in. 'Tell me.'

D'Or's purple rim-light, between his cap and main shell, seemed to take on an extra intensity. 'The new grid is possible. It really is possible, but it needs a particular human connection to trigger it, and right now. It must be now, between you and her, or we will be waiting until God knows when.'

That's a nice touch, thought Kit. First love, and now God? 'I thought you said you guys had it all figured out. Probability and all that.'

D'Or continued. 'Always a risk, Kit. Always a risk. We like to minimise that. Besides, and as I said, we like you.'

That was a mind-fuck, he thought. Robots that liked? 'And what do I have to process?'

'Your Julie.'

'What?'

'She was hit by an Ecobus this afternoon on her way back from work. Its proximity filters failed. That can happen. Anyway, she is in a coma at the Saint Micro Hospital and not expected to last another hour. If I can be specific, and circumstances do require it, there is a 99.8% likelihood that she will suffer a terminal stroke in two and a half minutes.'

'You're a bastard! You make this claim and I have no time to prove otherwise.'

'We need a connection. If you are willing to approach death, to risk termination, at the exact moment we throw the system over then we will have the trigger we need.'

'It doesn't make sense.'

'We don't need sense as you think of it, Kit. We need commitment.'

Kit lingered on this confusing mess of ideas. A robot was telling him to jump off a building because he had devised a plan that, unwittingly, contained the concept for a new way of running a city with less waste? A more organic way of life. Clean, symbiotic, equitable. How did this really relate to him and Julie in any way that made sense?

'Please watch, Kit? What is her favourite colour?'

'Um, purple.'

He watched as the haze over the city shifted into a beautiful purple.

'What is your favourite?'

'Blue.'

The purple hue distinctly shifted into a deep blue.

'I know it's hard to make the connection, Kit, but it is there. It is as natural as a tree and its roots. You have described a way to make a building partly into a living thing, and by extension a city also, but you need to jump or she is lost. And if you do not, then I think you will also be lost. If you do, you will join her and you will both be saved.'

'The sky thing?'

'The sky changes colour because the network you wanted is already there, and it contains more power than you could dream of. It is in the air and the earth, always has been. We have been listening and adapting and now we can make this happen. We are servers. There will be enough for everyone and at no cost. The biosystem you call Earth will give what it can but only that.'

'Why me?'

'Very existential, and a good question. We identified four people who have unwittingly been providing what was needed for this concept. None of them knew they were part of a team but it was most likely that one of them would also comprehend what was needed when the time came, even if we explained it in this crude manner. Because of Julie, it happened to be you. I hope you will understand why it had to be a surprise here, and suddenly, but we did not choose for her to be struck down.'

Kit felt that his days of moving gradually and comfortably from one step to another had been an illusion, someone else's life. What was time? The only things that mattered were ideas, his understanding — however wayward that might be — of how things 'worked'. And he was meshed into that somehow. Ultimately, he was still the one making the choice whatever the truth.

'You say now.'

'At this moment. Or more precisely in twenty seconds. I can count down if you like. In fact, it is better if I do.'

Kit put one foot on the ledge. 'And she is in a coma, and this will save her?'

'I know it. The bridge you make will be the trigger. You both will live.'

'How much longer?'

'Ten seconds.'

Kit lifted the other foot up onto the edge. Ten more seconds of me, he thought. Fewer now that I am counting them away. Is this all I have? The dwindling me?

Julie.

'Now,' said d'Or.

'D'Or. You would not lie?'

'Now.'

Kit jumped.

ACKNOWLEDGEMENTS

The author wishes to acknowledge the following for their support and for previously publishing work included in this book:

The Adelaide Review

The Advertiser

City Tales of Strangeness and Beauty

Spiny Babbler

ALSO BY STEVE EVANS

POETRY
Adult Fiction

Algebra

Animal Instincts

Bonetown

Edison Doesn't Invent the Car

Luminous Fruit

Taking Shape

Useful Translations

EDITED FICTION AND POETRY
Another Universe (ed. with Kate Deller-Evans)

Best of Friends: the first 30 years of the Friendly Street Poets
      (ed. with Kate Deller-Evans)

Corridors: Words on the Ward (ed. with Kate Deller-Evans)

NONFICTION
Balancing Act: The Creative Writing Pathway to
      Understanding Accounting (with Lee Parker)

Lift Off! an introductory course in creative writing (with Kate
      Deller-Evans)

ABOUT THE AUTHOR

Steve Evans coordinated the Creative Writing Program at Flinders University (Adelaide) for several years. His broad output includes poetry, general adult fiction, romance, detective fiction, and nonfiction.

Steve also reviews live music, stage performances and movies; is a long-standing literary editor; a fiction reader for *Overland*; and is a past member of several literary festival committees and arts panels.

He has been a writer-in-residence in Australia, New Zealand, Singapore, and Japan.

Also from TRUTH SERUM PRESS

https://truthserumpress.net/catalogue/

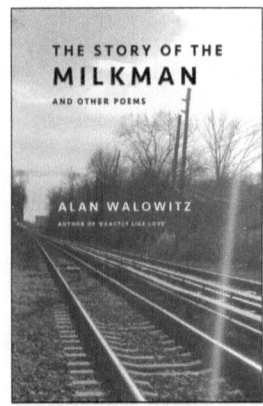  

- *The Story of the Milkman* by Alan Walowitz
  978-1-925536-76-8 (paperback) 978-1-925536-77-5 (eBook)
- *Minotaur and Other Stories* by Salvatore Difalco
  978-1-925536-79-9 (paperback) 978-1-925536-80-5 (eBook)
- *The Book of Acrostics* by John Lambremont, Sr.
  978-1-925536-52-2 (paperback) 978-1-925536-53-9 (eBook)

- *Square Pegs* by Rob Walker
  978-1-925536-62-1 (paperback) 978-1-925536-63-8 (eBook)
- *Cheat Sheets* by Edward O'Dwyer
  978-1-925536-60-7 (paperback) 978-1-925536-61-4 (eBook)
- *The Crazed Wind* by Nod Ghosh
  978-1-925536-58-4 (paperback) 978-1-925536-59-1 (eBook)

Also from TRUTH SERUM PRESS

https://truthserumpress.net/catalogue/

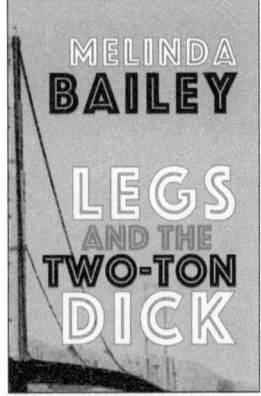  

- *Legs and the Two-Ton Dick* by Melinda Bailey
  978-1-925536-37-9 (paperback) 978-1-925536-38-6 (eBook)
- *Dollhouse Masquerade* by Samuel E. Cole
  978-1-925536-43-0 (paperback) 978-1-925536-44-7 (eBook)
- *Kiss Kiss* by Paul Beckman
  978-1-925536-21-8 (paperback) 978-1-925536-22-5 (eBook)

  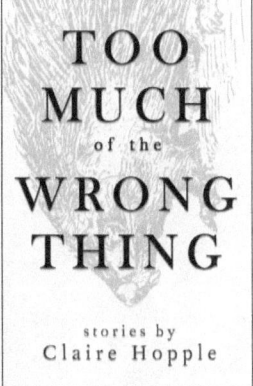

- *Inklings* by Irene Buckler
  978-1-925536-41-6 (paperback) 978-1-925536-42-3 (eBook)
- *On the Bitch* by Matt Potter
  978-1-925536-45-4 (paperback) 978-1-925536-46-1 (eBook)
- *Too Much of the Wrong Thing* by Claire Hopple
  978-1-925536-33-1 (paperback) 978-1-925536-34-8 (eBook)

Also from TRUTH SERUM PRESS

https://truthserumpress.net/catalogue/

- *Track Tales* by Mercedes Webb-Pullman
  978-1-925536-35-5 (paperback) 978-1-925536-36-2 (eBook)
- *Luck and Other Truths* by Richard Mark Glover
  978-1-925101-77-5 (paperback) 978-1-925536-04-1 (eBook)
- *Hello Berlin!* by Jason S. Andrews
  978-1-925536-11-9 (paperback) 978-1-925536-12-6 (eBook)

 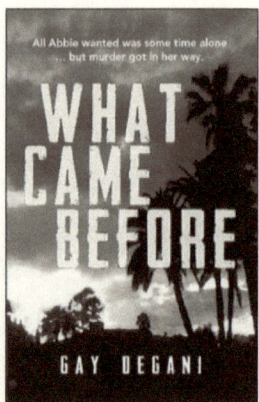 

- *Deer Michigan* by Jack C. Buck
  978-1-925536-25-6 (paperback) 978-1-925536-26-3 (eBook)
- *What Came Before* by Gay Degani
  978-1-925536-05-8 (paperback) 978-1-925536-06-5 (eBook)
- *Rain Check* by Levi Andrew Noe
  978-1-925536-09-6 (paperback) 978-1-925536-10-2 (eBook)